HEARTWARMING INSPIRATIONAL ROMANCE

Love

D0017167

Tides of Hope

Irene Hannon

Lighthouse
L A N E

Steeple
Hill®

GRIFFIN

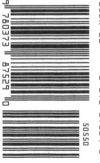
ISBN-13:978-0-373-87529-0
ISBN-10: 0-373-87529-0

LOVE INSPIRED® TITLES AVAILABLE THIS MONTH:

LIATMIFC0509

Spending time with Kate was not a good idea.

With each encounter, her appeal grew. And that was scary. At least the ride home was short, Craig thought, as he drove his car through the pouring rain.

"It's the next street on the right. Lighthouse Lane."

Kate directed him to a small clapboard cottage tucked into the tiny dead-end street.

"Thanks for the lift. I really appreciate it."

"It was my pleasure." The rain continued to beat against the car, the water isolating them from the outside world.

As he looked at her, he suddenly had the urge to touch her hair. To smooth away the shadows under her eyes. To assure her she didn't have to face her problems alone.

Where that urge came from, he had no idea. All he knew was that it threatened to shatter the control he'd mastered as a rescue swimmer. He needed that control. Nothing—and no one—had ever managed to shake it as quickly as Kate. Worse, she'd done it without even trying....

Books by Irene Hannon

Love Inspired

*Home for the Holidays
*A Groom of Her Own
*A Family to Call Her Own
It Had to Be You
One Special Christmas
The Way Home
Never Say Goodbye
Crossroads

**The Best Gift
**Gift from the Heart
**The Unexpected Gift
All Our Tomorrows
The Family Man
Rainbow's End
†From This Day Forward
†A Dream To Share
†Where Love Abides
Apprentice Father
††Tides of Hope

*Vows
**Sisters & Brides
†Heartland Homecomings
††Lighthouse Lane

IRENE HANNON

who writes both romance and romantic suspense, is the author of more than twenty-five novels. Her books have been honored with both the coveted RITA® Award from Romance Writers of America (the "Oscar" of romantic fiction) and the Reviewers' Choice Award from *Romantic Times BOOKreviews* magazine. More than 1 million copies of her novels have been sold worldwide.

A former corporate communications executive with a Fortune 500 company, Irene now writes full-time. In her spare time, she enjoys singing, long walks, cooking, gardening and spending time with family. She and her husband make their home in Missouri.

For more information about her and her books, Irene invites you to visit her Web site at www.irenehannon.com.

Tides of Hope
Irene Hannon

Steeple
Hill®

Published by Steeple Hill Books™

STEEPLE HILL BOOKS

Steeple
Hill®

PLEASE RECYCLE
THIS PRODUCT IS RECYCLABLE

Recycling programs
for this product may
not exist in your area.

ISBN-13: 978-0-373-87529-0
ISBN-10:   0-373-87529-0

TIDES OF HOPE

Blessed are those who mourn,
for they shall be comforted.
—*Matthew 5:4*

To my mother, Dorothy Hannon—
With loving memories of a very special bird's nest
that always graces my Christmas tree...
and The Good Life

With special thanks to the following individuals
for their generous assistance:

BMC Terrill J. Malvesti, United States
Coast Guard; Julie & Karsten Reinemo,
Topspin Sportfishing Charters;
Erika Mooney, The 'Sconset Trust;
Michael Galvin, Nantucket Chamber of Commerce.

Chapter One

"Sorry to interrupt, sir. But I've got a hot one for you."

Swiveling his desk chair away from the foggy view of Nantucket Harbor, Lieutenant Craig Cole looked up from the boat-hours report he'd just started reading and gave his executive petty officer his full attention. "What's up?"

"A complaint, sir. From the owner of one of the local charter fishing operations, who isn't too happy about a safety citation we issued this afternoon. The captain asked to speak with you, but you were at that special Conservation Commission meeting. I'm not making any headway, so now that you're back I thought you might want to take over."

The subtle twitch of his aide's lips put Craig on alert. Boatswain's Mate First Class Ben Barlow had been stationed on Nantucket for two years, and he'd been an invaluable—if slightly irreverent—source of information since Craig's arrival four weeks ago, guiding him through several rocky passages. Another one seemed to be looming on the horizon.

"Okay, Barlow. What's the story?"

The man walked into the office and handed over a copy of the citation. "It's pretty straightforward. Expired flares."

Craig scanned the document. The vessel was an older boat,

a thirty-one-foot Wellcraft Suncruiser named the *Lucy Sue*. Although it was equipped with a sufficient number of flares, they were out-of-date. The inspection had been done by the station's newest—and youngest—crew member, but Craig considered the man to be dependable and conscientious.

"This looks in order. What's the problem?"

His aide's lip twitch gave way to a grin. "The captain says we're being hard-nosed. The flares are only a month out-of-date, and she says everyone knows they're good for at least six months longer than the expiration date. However, she claims she did intend to replace them before resuming operation this season."

She. Craig checked the name on the citation. Katherine MacDonald. Was the captain's gender the source of Barlow's amusement?

Lowering the sheet of paper, Craig appraised his aide. "I don't care what she says. This is a clear violation of regulations."

"I explained that to her, sir. But she isn't backing down." The man tried to stifle his grin. Failed.

Craig's eyes narrowed. "Do you know this woman?"

"No, sir. But I know Chief Medart had a lot of respect for her."

From what he'd heard about his predecessor, Senior Chief Sandra Medart was a solid officer. He'd found no evidence of a lax operation during his brief tenure, though it was more laid-back than he was accustomed to, after his past three years at headquarters in Washington, where protocol and procedures reigned supreme.

"Are you suggesting that Chief Medart let personal feelings influence her enforcement of the law, Barlow?"

"No, sir." The man's reply was prompt. "But Captain Mac-Donald has lived on the island her whole life, and she's been doing fishing charters for at least a dozen years. I believe she's descended from an old island whaling family. Her roots here are deep."

"That doesn't exempt her from the law."

"No, sir. She's waiting in my office, sir." The man inclined his head toward the door.

Listening to an unjustified tirade hadn't been part of Craig's Friday afternoon agenda on this last day of March, but he'd expected some backlash once Nantucketers got wind of the beefed-up inspection program he'd implemented earlier in the week. And PR was part of the job in a command post—especially this one, as Admiral Paul Gleason had reminded him when he'd called to tell Craig his request for reassignment had been granted. This would be his first test, Craig supposed—smoothing ruffled feathers without backing down from his firm position on safety-regulation enforcement.

"Send her in."

"Yes, sir." His aide retreated as far as the door. "One word of warning, sir. She has red hair. And a temper to go with it." Making no attempt to hide his grin, he closed the door behind him.

At the petty officer's parting remark, Craig took a moment to ready himself for the coming exchange. He'd dealt with plenty of distraught people during his career. Handling a small-time charter-fishing boat captain should be a piece of cake—red hair notwithstanding. He'd diffuse her anger by remaining calm, cool and sympathetic, he decided. And he'd do his best to keep the encounter as nonconfrontational and pleasant as possible.

But thirty seconds later, when Katherine MacDonald stormed across his office to his desk, planted her hands on her hips and pinned him with a glare, his hopes of a cordial discussion disintegrated. For a woman so small—Craig estimated her height at no more than five foot three—she projected as intimidating a presence as any of the hard-as-nails instructors he'd encountered during his Coast Guard career.

As he rose under the scrutiny of her turbulent, flashing

green eyes, a memory of the worst squall he'd ever encountered suddenly flashed through his mind. It had happened back in his early days as a rescue swimmer, when he'd been stationed in Alaska. A small cargo vessel out of Kodiak had lost propulsion and drifted onto the rocks at Cape Trinity, forcing the three crewmen to ditch into the icy, churning sea. As Craig had waited, legs dangling over the edge of the Jayhawk, for the thumbs-up from the flight mechanic to drop into the roiling swells, he'd known the dicey, dangerous mission would be forever etched in his memory.

For some disconcerting reason, he felt the same way about this encounter with Katherine MacDonald.

Nevertheless, he did his best to summon up a smile, determined to try and salvage the situation. "Ms. MacDonald, won't you have a seat?" He gestured to one of the chairs across from his desk.

"I prefer to stand. This won't take long."

Her curt reply, along with the bristling rage radiating across the expanse of desk between them, left him little maneuvering room. He'd planned to lead off with some small talk designed to soothe her ire, but it was obvious the woman across from him was in no mood for chitchat. Better to plunge in and get this over with.

"I understand you have a concern about the safety citation that was issued this afternoon." He kept his tone polite and conversational.

The color rose on her cheeks, drawing his attention to the faint dusting of freckles across the bridge of her nose and the fine lines at the corners of her eyes. The wind and sun could have produced those creases, Craig knew, but the faint smudges of fatigue under the sweep of her lower lashes suggested that outdoor living might not be their only source.

Yanking the crumpled citation out of the pocket of her slicker, she tossed it on his desk, a few tendrils of fiery hair escaping from the clip at her nape to quiver around her face. "This is ridiculous."

Despite his best effort to remain conciliatory, a note of defensiveness crept into Craig's voice. "I don't think so. Your flares are expired."

"They last longer than the expiration date. You know that as well as I do. And I was going to replace them before the season opened anyway."

"I'm sorry, Ms. MacDonald. But safety regulations are in place for a reason. And I don't take them lightly."

"Neither do I." Her color deepened as she glowered at him. "Look. You're new here. Fresh out of Washington, from what I hear. This is real life, Lieutenant, where rules aren't quite as cut and dried. I've spent most of my thirty-eight years on this island. A lot of it on the water. I've operated a charter fishing business for fourteen of those years. I don't take chances with the sea, and I would never put anyone who steps onto my boat in danger."

She fisted her hands on her hips, her lips tightening. "Furthermore, I have never been cited for any safety violations, and the *Lucy Sue* has always had a VSC decal from the Coast Guard. I was only taking her for a quick run when that wet-behind-the-ears Coastie pulled alongside for a surprise inspection. And instead of listening to reason, he gave me that." She jabbed a finger at the document on Craig's desk. "He even inspected my life jackets. One by one! Under your orders, I presume."

A hot flush rose on Craig's neck. He didn't appreciate this woman's belligerent attitude, nor her insulting tone. He didn't deserve to be taken to task for doing his job. If previous station commanders had overlooked expired equipment, that was their problem.

"I'm not sure why you're so upset, Ms. MacDonald. All you have to do is buy a few new flares and the problem goes away. They're not expensive."

"It's not the cost. It's the principle. And for your information, the problem doesn't go away. A black mark like this on my record will hurt my business. Charter fishing is my livelihood, Lieutenant. This is a very competitive market, and potential customers do check safety ratings." She put her fingertips on his desk and leaned forward, narrowing the gap between their faces to a mere fifteen inches, undaunted by his distinct height advantage as she tipped her chin up to lock gazes with him. "I want mine fixed."

Craig might not agree with her stance, but he had to admire her spunk. "What did you have in mind, Ms. MacDonald?"

Her resolute expression hardened. "Here's the deal. I'll get the stupid flares sooner rather than later, even though we both know the ones I have are perfectly fine right now. But I want this citation—" she swatted at the crumpled sheet without breaking eye contact "—wiped off my record."

Expunging a legitimate safety citation wasn't common protocol. And the challenge sparking in the charter captain's green irises told Craig she knew that.

His first inclination was to refuse her request. The rule book would back him up one hundred percent.

But at close range, what he saw in her eyes made him hesitate. Determination, certainly, and strong will. Plus a good measure of anger and impatience. But it was the deep-seated worry and the echo of profound sadness in their depths that held him back. This was a woman who had endured more than her share of sorrow, who'd been knocked down, pushed to the limits and was fighting to hold on. To survive.

A lot of people might not pick all that up, Craig supposed. Perhaps *most* people wouldn't. But it was clear to him. Every bit of it. Because he knew how hard it was to forge ahead despite the harsh blows life dealt. He'd been there. Was *still* there.

As the silence between them lengthened, a sudden flicker of uncertainty crept into Katherine MacDonald's eyes. Then, abruptly, she backed off several feet. Thrusting her hands into the pockets of her slicker, she sent him a wary look.

Interesting, Craig mused. This feisty woman didn't mind in-your-face confrontations to protect her business. But let someone get too close on a personal level and her strategy was to beat a hasty retreat.

Tipping up her chin, she made a valiant attempt to recapture her earlier bravado. But her challenge came off more distraught than defiant. "Well? Do we have a deal?"

"Let me think about it."

She blinked. Sucked in a breath. Blew it out. "Okay. Your people know where to find me. In the meantime, I'll get the flares."

Turning on her heel, she exited without another word.

For a full minute, Craig remained standing behind his desk, trying to figure out what had just happened. He felt the same as he always had after emerging from a perilous rescue mission. Nerve endings tingling. Pulse pounding. Lungs pumping.

In his rescue-swimmer days, however, it hadn't taken long for the adrenaline rush to subside. But that wasn't happening today. Instead, he was swamped by an odd mix of emotions that left him feeling unsettled, off balance—and irritated. He *never* let emotion affect him on the job. As a rescue swimmer, there'd been no room for it. Succumbing to even a few seconds of debilitating fear could have meant the difference between life and death for himself or the victims he'd been sent to save. Nor had it had a place during his tenure as controller of a search and rescue command center, where deployment decisions were based on the pure facts and figures of the Mayday. And it had been easy to keep emotion in check in Washington. Shuffling papers had engendered little more than mind-numbing boredom.

As for emotion in his personal life, he'd kept that carefully tucked away these past three years, as well, leaving his days dull—but livable.

That had all changed in the past ten minutes. Emotion could be Katherine MacDonald's middle name, Craig concluded. Hers hadn't just run high; they'd exploded. Even now, in her absence, the room continued to vibrate with them. He doubted the word dull was in her vocabulary—or in anyone's who came into contact with her.

A discreet knock sounded on the door, and when Craig responded, Barlow stepped inside, his grin still in place. "Checking on survivors, sir."

Ignoring his aide's comment, Craig picked up the pristine copy of the safety citation he'd scanned earlier and handed it over, leaving the crumpled version untouched on his desk. "See that this is held for a couple of days before we file it."

"Yes, sir."

The amusement in the man's voice wasn't lost on Craig, and he felt warmth once again steal up his neck. Fixing the executive petty officer with a steely look, Craig folded his arms across his chest. "Is there a problem?"

To Barlow's credit, his demeanor instantly grew more serious. That was why Craig tolerated the man's slight impertinence. Not only did he balance it with a likable manner and razor-sharp skills, he knew where to draw the line.

"No, sir."

His aide beat a hasty retreat, and Craig walked to the window to survey the harbor. It was far emptier than it would be in a couple of months, but a fair number of boats were in residence—including Katherine MacDonald's. Strange. Half an hour ago, he hadn't known the woman existed. Yet in the course of one brief conversation, she'd managed to awaken emotions in him that were best left undisturbed.

As for his plans for a nice, relaxing weekend—they, too, had been disrupted. Also thanks to one certain red-haired fishing boat captain.

* * *

"Mommy, Mommy, Mrs. Shaw and me baked cookies! Chocolate chip!"

As Kate bent to hug her daughter, she glanced over the four-year-old's shoulder toward the stocky, gray-haired woman behind her. "I bet that was fun, honey. It sounds like you had a good afternoon."

The woman gave a reassuring nod. "Maddie and I had a fine afternoon."

Some of the tension in Kate's shoulders eased. But it would take a lot longer for the rest of it to dissipate, thanks to her unpleasant encounter less than an hour ago with a certain lieutenant.

"You seem stressed, my dear." The older woman gave Kate a discerning perusal. "Why don't you have a cup of tea before you head home?"

A whisper of a smile tugged at her lips. "I ought to go next door to The Devon Rose if I want tea instead of taking advantage of your hospitality."

"That would be more elegant, no question about it. Heather serves a wonderful proper British tea." Then Edith winked. "But I guarantee she won't offer you home-baked chocolate chip cookies. As for taking advantage…that's nonsense. We're neighbors, for goodness' sake. You've listened to me vent plenty of times. I'm happy to return the favor."

"Is it that obvious I need to?"

"In a word…yes. Problems with the *Lucy Sue?*"

"Minor compared to my problems with Lieutenant Craig Cole."

"You met the invisible man?" Interest sparked in the older woman's eyes.

"Who's the invisible man?"

Her daughter's question reminded Kate how little the youngster missed—and of the need for prudence in her presence when discussing grown-up topics.

"It's kind of a joke, honey. No one has seen very much of the new commander at the Coast Guard station, so people call him the invisible man."

"Maybe he's busy."

"I expect that's the reason."

"Maddie, why don't you finish building your castle in the sunroom while your mommy and I have some tea?" Edith interjected. "After we're done, you can tell us a story about the people who live there."

"Okay."

As Maddie skipped off, Kate shook her head. "Talk about little pitchers."

"She doesn't miss much, that's for sure."

"No more problems today?"

"Not a one. She's fine, Kate. Come on, let's have that tea."

"Could we make it coffee instead?"

Edith grinned. "Heather still hasn't converted you, I see."

"It's a lost cause."

"She's made inroads with me. But I still like my coffee, too. You're on." Edith led the way toward her early American-style kitchen, pulling two mugs from pegs on the wall.

"Where's Chester?" Kate took a seat at the familiar hickory table that had hosted more than its share of gab sessions and propped her chin in her palm.

"In the garden, finishing up the renovations on the guest cottage." She shook her head as she bustled about the homey room. "I'm not convinced it will be ready to rent out this season, though. My good husband has been futzing around with it for months, and the tourists will be descending before we know it."

"And life will get even busier." Kate sighed and selected a cookie from the plate on the table.

After pulling a pitcher of cream from the refrigerator, Edith turned a keen eye toward her Lighthouse Lane neighbor. "Do I detect a hint of discouragement in that comment?"

Forcing her lips into a smile, Kate shrugged. "Maybe."

"That's not like you. You've always kept a positive attitude despite problems that would have made most people cave long ago."

"You and Chester can take a lot of credit for that. If you hadn't agreed to watch Maddie while I work, and if Chester hadn't stepped in as my first mate, I doubt I'd have made it."

"Yes, you would. You're a survivor, Kate MacDonald. But even the best of us can get discouraged on a bad day. And yours sounds like a doozy." She dropped her volume. "Starting with Maddie's asthma attack at four in the morning."

"It wasn't a great beginning," Kate conceded, angling her head toward the window-rimmed room Chester had added to the back of the kitchen. Maddie was busy with her blocks and oblivious to the adult conversation, the panic-filled attack in the wee hours of the morning, the tears, the nebulizer treatment already a distant memory.

Kate wished the same was true for her. But after each episode, the agony of watching her daughter struggle for air and the feeling of desperate helplessness that twisted her stomach into knots stayed with her. Sometimes guilt was thrown in for good measure, too. Like now.

Setting aside the uneaten cookie, Kate massaged her forehead with her fingertips. "The thing is, I know the triggers for her attacks. I should have taken her ski mask yesterday when we went grocery shopping. She breathed too much cold air."

"Don't beat yourself up, Kate. It was a beautiful day until that front decided to drop in unannounced."

"Nantucket weather is unpredictable. I should have been prepared."

Edith filled both mugs from the coffeemaker on the counter and took a seat at a right angle to her guest. "Only one person who walked on this earth was perfect, Kate. And He doesn't expect anyone to repeat that feat. He just expects us to try our best. And you always do that. This morning's asthma episode is history. Let's move on to what happened today."

On stressful days like this, Kate was grateful for Edith's practical, no-nonsense approach. It always helped her regain perspective. Taking a fortifying sip of the hot brew, she told her neighbor about the citation.

"That's a technicality." Edith waved a hand in dismissal. "You replace the flares every year. Besides, they last longer than that."

"That's what I told the by-the-book lieutenant, who instituted the beefed-up inspection program. I paid him a visit to express my...displeasure."

Edith quirked an eyebrow. "How did that go?"

As the scene replayed in Kate's mind, she frowned and ran a finger around the rim of her mug. Warmth seeped into the tip—and up the back of her neck. "Not very well. I suppose I might have been a bit...vocal...in my opinions."

Grinning, Edith took a sip of coffee. "I wish I'd been a fly on the wall."

The heat on Kate's neck rose to her cheek. The bane of redheads, she lamented. "Anyway, in the end I agreed to replace them right away if he erased the citation from my record. He said he'd think about it."

"Hmm. That's interesting." Edith stirred her coffee, her expression speculative. "What do you think convinced your by-the-book commander to consider overlooking the violation?"

It wasn't anything she'd said, that was for sure, Kate acknowledged. Whatever diplomacy skills she possessed had deserted her during their meeting. By the time she'd faced off with him across the desk and delivered her ultimatum, she'd expected him to refuse based on her attitude alone.

But then, out of the blue, his cobalt eyes had softened a fraction—telling her he'd seen far more than she'd wanted to reveal. Thrown by his ability to so easily breach the defenses around her heart, she'd backed off and escaped as fast as she could.

Still, if whatever he'd detected convinced him to cut her some slack, maybe it had been worth that brief exposure. Their paths weren't likely to cross very often once this was resolved. In fact, she'd do her best to ensure they didn't. No way did she want to risk experiencing that unsettling feeling of vulnerability again.

Realizing that Edith was waiting for a response, Kate cleared her throat. "I don't know why he eased off. I guess he had some second thoughts."

"Hmm." Edith tipped her head, and Kate shifted under her scrutiny, uncertain how to interpret the gleam in the woman's eye. "So what does the invisible man look like?"

Although she'd been too angry to pay much attention to his appearance, Kate had no problem summoning up an image of him. And *handsome* was the word that popped into her mind. Lean and toned, with broad shoulders and a powerful chest, he had a take-charge manner and a commanding bearing that radiated strength and competence.

"I didn't focus on his looks, Edith."

"Oh, come now. You must have noticed the basics. Height, hair color, age."

"Six one or two, I'd guess. Dark blond hair. Fortyish."

"Attractive?"

She shrugged and tried for nonchalance. "I suppose some women might think so."

"Are you one of them?"

Kate didn't like the twinkle in her neighbor's eye. Much to her dismay, for the past few months Edith had been introducing the subject of romance with increasing frequency. As usual, Kate discouraged her.

"He's not my type, Edith. And I'm not in the market anyway." She swallowed and looked down into the black depths of her coffee. "There was only one man for me."

The older woman reached out and covered Kate's hand with her own, all traces of humor vanishing from her voice. "Mac was one of a kind, Kate. No question about that. But he wouldn't want you to live the rest of your life alone if another man came along who was worthy of your love."

"No one could ever take his place, Edith. Besides, my life is crazy enough without adding romance to the mix." Gesturing toward the sunroom, she rose. "Let's go check on Maddie's castle, okay?" Without waiting for a response, she picked up her mug and moved away from the table.

But a few minutes later, as she and Edith listened to the youngster's imaginative story about the castle she'd constructed from her blocks, the most annoying thing happened.

Every time Maddie mentioned Prince Charming, an image of Lieutenant Craig Cole came to mind.

Chapter Two

By Sunday afternoon, Nantucket was living up to her nickname—The Gray Lady. But the dismal weather couldn't dampen Kate's upbeat mood. Thanks to Chester's magic touch with all things mechanical, the *Lucy Sue*'s sometimes-temperamental engine was purring along as her bow cut a wide swath through the choppy seas off Great Point. And despite another asthma attack in the middle of the night, Maddie had awakened with no ill effects.

Her skin tingling from the salt spray, Kate took a deep, cleansing breath of the bracing air. Nothing could be more relaxing than this, she concluded. And today was the perfect chance to enjoy it. Although she'd be making this trip twice daily with a boatful of amateur anglers once the season kicked off, their need for constant attention would leave her little opportunity to relish the grand view of the majestic whitewashed lighthouse and the long expanse of pristine beach backed by endless sky.

Today the outline of the tall, stately column was blurred by the gray mantle draped over the island, but the bright white light that flashed every five seconds made the tower easy to locate. In a world where very little could be counted on, Kate took comfort in that steady, consistent beacon. And she appreciated it most on days like this, when Nantucket's three lighthouses had the chance to do the job for which they were designed—guiding lost souls safely home.

In truth, Kate didn't mind the dreary weather. The view might be prettier on sunny summer days, when the heavens were deep blue and the sea sparkled as if it had been strewn with diamonds, but she felt a kinship with this wild, wind-swept speck of land no matter its wardrobe. Isolated by twenty-six miles of sea from the mainland, Nantucket was a place that bred strength, where self-reliance was a way of life and only the hardy survived.

Unlike summer people and day-trippers, who came to sample the unique rhythm of the island but whose lives pulsed to a beat far removed from these shores, the lives of year-rounders were inexorably linked to the cadence of the sea. It had been that way back in the bustling whaling days, and it was no different now. Only ten thousand people could claim the title of Nantucketer, and Kate was proud to be one of them.

Just as Mac had been.

Swallowing past the sudden lump in her throat, Kate blinked and checked her watch. Time to head back and pick up Maddie from Edith's. She didn't want to take advantage of her neighbor's generosity—or grow maudlin thinking about the man who'd filled her days with sunshine and whose loss had left an aching void in her heart.

As Kate swung the wheel to port and pointed the *Lucy Sue* back toward the harbor, she scanned the undulating sea, relishing the solitude. In two months, this prime fishing ground would be dotted with crafts of all sizes. Today she had the spot to herself.

Or did she?

A bobbing orange speck in the distance caught her eye, and she eased back on the throttle, squinting through the mist. It could be debris, she supposed. But she'd pulled more than her share of too-confident swimmers out of these waters and had learned long ago never to overestimate people's common sense.

Without taking her gaze off the spot where the orange speck kept disappearing among the swells, she felt for the binoculars secured within reaching distance of the helm. Fitting them to her eyes, she planted her feet in a wide, steadying stance and focused on the object.

In general, the seven-by-thirty magnification was sufficient for her needs. But today it couldn't overcome the obscuring combination of distance, mist and the rocking motion of the boat. All she could tell with any certainty was that the object was about fifty yards offshore and moving on a steady, purposeful course parallel to the beach.

Meaning it was alive.

And it wasn't a seal or a fish. Fluorescent orange wasn't in the marine life palette of Nantucket.

That left only one possibility.

It was human.

Shaking her head, Kate huffed out a breath. What kind of idiot would go for a dip off Great Point? These were dangerous swimming waters any time of year, let alone in early April, when the threat of hypothermia amplified the peril.

It was obvious the swimmer churning through the swells didn't understand the risks—or didn't consider them to be a problem. She didn't know which was worse. The former smacked of stupidity, the latter of arrogance. In either case, someone needed to pound some sense into the guy's head. And it *was* a guy. She was sure of that, even if the conclusion reeked of stereotypical sexism.

Compressing her lips into a grim line, Kate swung the *Lucy Sue* hard to starboard, shifted into full throttle and headed straight for the bobbing orange speck. Disgust and annoyance vied for top billing on her emotional chart, with impatience and frustration not far behind. Whoever she found cavorting in the heaving gray swells was about to get an earful.

One, two, three, four, five, breathe. One, two, three, four, five, breathe. One, two, three, four, five, breathe.

Encased in his neoprene wet suit, Craig cut through the swells with powerful, even strokes, propelling himself forward with strong, steady kicks of his flippers, oblivious to the forty-two-degree water. After all the missions he'd swum in the Arctic, this was a bathtub. The chop was distracting, and the riptide had been a tad annoying, but neither had disrupted his bilateral breathing rhythm. After fifteen minutes of steady swimming, he wasn't even winded.

As he sliced through the water, Craig counted each stroke as a victory over the intimidating marine conditions—and over his emotions. It had taken him two years to put so much as a toe in the ocean after the accident. He'd hated the sea with the same intensity he'd once loved it, his anger almost palpable. If it had been an enemy he could have gotten his hands around, he'd have choked the life out of it. Not the most Christian impulse, he knew, but that was how he'd felt.

Those potent feelings had prompted his request for a transfer from field duty to Washington. Hoping his fury and grief would ebb in a new environment, he'd planned to complete his twenty years of military service behind a desk, as far removed from his previous life as possible. And retirement wasn't far in the future. Because he'd enlisted right out of college, he'd be able to wrap up his Coast Guard career as a relatively young man. Only three more years to go.

To his relief, the time and distance provided by three years of desk duty had eased his sorrow and mitigated his rage— to some degree. But much to his surprise, as his hate had begun to recede, his love of the sea had resurfaced. He'd fought it fiercely, overwhelmed by guilt, unable to understand how he could yearn to return to the very thing that had robbed his life of joy.

Until Paul Gleason had helped him make an uneasy peace with his conflicting feelings.

The admiral had come upon him one night last fall, seated in his windowless office in Washington behind tall stacks of reports awaiting his review. Craig had been trying all week to make some headway on them, but by Friday he'd done little more than riffle through a few.

Annoyed by his inability to focus, he'd been determined to stay all night if necessary to deal with the pile of official documents. No way had he wanted them waiting for him on Monday morning. But neither had he relished his self-imposed assignment. Paul's unexpected appearance at his office door at the end of the day had been a welcome reprieve.

"Looks like you're planning to burn the proverbial midnight oil."

At the admiral's greeting, Craig had summoned up a smile. "If that's what it takes to empty my in basket."

"What about Vicki?"

A wave of guilt had washed over him, and Craig had picked up a stack of papers on his desk and tapped them into a neat, precise pile. His personal life might be a mess, but at least he could keep his desk tidy. "The nanny will put her to bed."

He'd waited for Paul to comment, to add another layer of guilt to the load he already carried over his lackluster approach to fatherhood. And he deserved it, Craig had acknowledged. For all his heroic work on the job, he was no hero when it came to raising his daughter. That, too, had begun to eat at him.

To his relief, Paul had let the subject pass. Instead, the admiral had surveyed the stack of reports and given a low whistle, arching his trademark shaggy white eyebrows. "You could be here till morning."

"Tell me about it. How have you managed to deal with this kind of stuff day after day for all these years? I'm not even convinced it's written in English." In public, he and the admiral—his mentor since their days at Air Station Kodiak well over a decade ago—observed military protocol. Off duty, their relationship had evolved into a comfortable friendship.

A rueful chuckle had rumbled in the older man's chest. Dropping into the chair across from Craig's desk, he'd run his hand over his close-cropped white hair. "I'm afraid it comes with the rank. But I must confess there are days I wish I was back in Kodiak. Once the sea grabs hold of you, she never lets go."

Casting a shrewd eye at the younger officer, the admiral had leaned back in his chair. "By the way...I have some news. I'm retiring the first of the year. Mag and I are going to take up full-time residence in our little cottage in Maine and go sailing every chance we get."

The announcement shouldn't have surprised Craig. After thirty-five years of military service, Paul deserved his retirement. Yet the news had left him with mixed feelings.

"I'm happy for you, Paul. And more than a little envious."

"You're too young to retire." Paul had folded his hands over his stomach, its girth a bit wider since their Kodiak days. "Or were you referring to my return to the sea?"

Not much got past the admiral, Craig had acknowledged. Picking up a pen, he'd tapped it against his palm as he'd weighed his response. "There are days lately when this—" he'd swept his hand around the office "—gets on my nerves and I think about the sea. But I asked for this transfer. I shouldn't complain."

"You needed an escape then. Maybe you don't anymore." Paul had steepled his fingers and given Craig a steady look. "You know, I'll be here through December. If a request for a transfer came through, I'd be inclined to give it a favorable review."

Shaking his head, Craig had raked his fingers through his hair. "I shouldn't even consider it."

"Why not?"

"After what happened…how could I want to be around the sea?"

The hint of a smile had touched the admiral's lips. "Love is a strange thing, Craig. Whether for a woman or for the sea. You don't like everything about her all the time. Sometimes she does things that infuriate you. There are days you're tempted to walk away. But you never stop loving her. Not if it's real. That's how love works."

Several moments of silence had ticked by while Craig considered the admiral's comment. "I don't know, Paul."

The man had stood and rested a hand on the tall stack of reports. "Well, I do. You don't belong behind this desk. You never did. You've done a great job here, but this isn't where you should finish your career. Think about it. A change like that could be good for you—and Vicki. She's only four, Craig. She needs you."

In the end, after weeks of soul searching, Craig had come to the same conclusion. Although he hadn't understood his jumbled feelings about the sea, he'd asked for a transfer back to the field. To a station on the other side of the country from Hawaii, hoping a new setting would give him a fresh start with his life—and with his daughter. The opening on Nantucket had fit the bill.

An icy smack in the face from an unruly wave brought Craig abruptly back to the present. Caught unaware, he sucked in a mouthful of water. Coughed. Lost his rhythm.

Anger surged through him, and he swam with renewed energy, arms slashing through the water, attacking the swells. He'd let the sea surprise him, score a point. Bad mistake. One he'd vowed never to let happen again. His last mistake had cost him too—

"Hey! Hey, you!"

At the shouted summons, Craig broke his rhythm again, this time on purpose. Riding the swells, he lifted his head and checked for the source.

The name of the boat rocking on the waves a few yards away clicked into focus first. *Lucy Sue.*

Meaning the human hurricane couldn't be far behind.

Taking a deep breath, Craig looked higher. Sure enough, the voice belonged to none other than Katherine MacDonald. And she was in a snit once again, judging by her ruddy color and tense posture as she glared down at him, her wind-tossed red hair whipping about her face.

The full blast of her fury was coming. He knew that. He'd already had a sample of her temper, and the signs were all there. But instead of using the lull before the storm to brace himself, he found his thoughts wandering to Grace O'Malley, the legendary Irish pirate queen. Somehow he had a feeling she'd looked a lot like Katherine MacDonald.

"…recreational swimming area!"

The tail end of her comment interrupted his musings. "What?"

"I said, are you crazy? This is not a recreational swimming area!" She had to yell to be heard above the hum of the engine and the waves slapping against the side of the boat.

"I'm fine," he called back.

"You can't be fine! The water's freezing! And there's a bad riptide here. You need to get back to shore!" She flicked her hand toward the beach, as if shooing a recalcitrant puppy back from the edge of a busy street.

It was obvious she didn't recognize him. But why should she? His wet suit, swim cap and goggles left very few identifying features exposed.

As he bobbed on the swells, he considered his options. The path of least resistance would be to remain anonymous, acquiesce and retreat to the beach. That would be the smart thing to do. He'd been about ready to head toward shore anyway.

Instead, prompted by some impulse he couldn't identify, he lifted his goggles and settled them on top of the orange swim cap. "I can handle this sea, Ms. MacDonald."

Her reaction as his identity became apparent was reward enough for his rash action. Seeing Katherine MacDonald shocked speechless was, he suspected, a rare treat.

Unfortunately, it was short-lived.

"I don't believe this! You, of all people, should know better than to swim in seas like this! Alone, no less! And you cited *me* for a safety violation?"

He'd known she'd come back with a zinger. She hadn't disappointed him.

"I'm trained to swim in worse conditions than these. And I'm well-equipped."

She dismissed his explanation with a curt flip of her hand. "That may be true, but no one in their right mind would put themselves into dangerous conditions without cause. Do you have a death wish or something?"

For some reason, her question jolted him. He knew it was an exaggeration, meant to drive home her point, yet it left him feeling uneasy. And no longer interested in prolonging their verbal sparring match.

Pulling his goggles back over his eyes, he prepared to resume his swim.

The red-haired spitfire must have sensed his intent because she called out again. "I can't in good conscience leave anyone alone in these waters, especially in this weather."

He checked her out over his shoulder as he treaded water, buoyant on the rising swells. She was still standing by the side of the boat, gripping the rail, watching him.

Ignoring her comment, he resumed his course, swimming parallel to the shore.

Thirty seconds later, he heard the hum of her boat behind him.

Craig kept swimming for two more minutes, the boat pacing him. She wasn't backing down. No surprise there, he supposed. And he didn't relish company on his solitary swims. Besides, he'd stayed out as long as he'd planned, and the cold seeping through his neoprene insulation was beginning to get uncomfortable.

Altering his course, he aimed for shore. Let Katherine MacDonald assume she'd won the battle. He knew better. Had she caught him at the beginning of his swim instead of the end, he'd have put up with the audience and she'd have found herself tooling around in the *Lucy Sue* far longer as she discovered he could be as strong-willed as she was.

That revelation wasn't going to happen today.

But he had a strong suspicion it was coming.

As the lieutenant changed direction and headed for shore, Kate let out a long, relieved breath. Good. Had he balked, she wasn't at all confident she'd have won the skirmish. Yet the rule-bound commander didn't strike her as the kind of man prone to capitulation. So why had he given in?

The answer, she grudgingly acknowledged, was clear.

He'd been ready to call it a day anyway.

Meaning her victory was hollow.

Kate planted her fists on her hips and watched as he surged through the swells with powerful strokes, doing her best to stifle the flicker of admiration fanned to life by his masterful physical control and his command of the water. Just because he was a good swimmer didn't mean he should be taking chances by venturing into hazardous seas alone. It was folly to feel invincible around the ocean, no matter how strong or well-equipped you were. And a Coast Guard lieutenant should know that. Taking him to task for his irresponsible actions had been more than justified.

The instant he emerged from the water, Kate once more swung the *Lucy Sue* to port and headed home. And as the boat plowed through the waves, she forced herself to switch gears and focus on the pleasant evening ahead. She and Maddie were planning to indulge in a pizza, followed by a movie of her daughter's choice. No doubt her current favorite, *The Lion King*. They'd seen it four times already, but Kate didn't mind. Cuddling with her daughter under an afghan, a cozy fire burning in the grate, was about the most comforting way she could imagine to spend a chilly evening.

Only one thing would be missing from that picture of contentment, she reflected, the salt from the spray reminding her of the taste of tears. Mac wouldn't be with them. How he would have loved an evening like that! With him, however, it would have been impromptu, a spontaneous celebration rather than a planned event. He'd had a remarkable gift for turning ordinary days into special occasions, his infectious *joie de vivre* and go-with-the-flow attitude carrying everyone along with him.

Kate could imagine what tonight would be like if he were here. Instead of pizza, he might suggest chocolate chip waffles. Rather than sitting on the couch, he might drag out their folding chairs, make popcorn and have them all pretend they were at the old hall in 'Sconset that showed family movies in the summer. And he might resurrect their vintage video of *The Sound of Music* and encourage them all to sing along, his off-key baritone and contagious laugh ringing through the house.

Life with Mac had been one grand adventure, Kate recalled, her lips softening into a melancholy smile. Flexible, agreeable, always upbeat, he was a man who'd lived—and loved—with an abandon that had taken her breath away. Without him, she felt as she had as a child waking up the day after Christmas, the excitement and anticipation of the previous day replaced by a sense that life for the next 364 days would be dull, dull, dull.

Though Kate's world had been graced by the presence of Dennis "Mac" MacDonald far too briefly, she would always be grateful to him for their days together. And for teaching her by example to embrace life—and not sweat the small stuff. She'd struggled at times with that during the past few years, but at least she kept trying.

The stiff, stuffy lieutenant she'd left on Great Point would do well to learn that lesson, too, Kate thought, her smile fading as her hands tightened on the helm. He seemed focused *only* on the small stuff. Such pettiness was an unlikable trait to begin with, and even less endearing because it had caused her nothing but problems. The commander's insistence on following the letter of the law—whether it made sense or not—was maddening.

Calm down, Kate, she counseled herself, easing her grip on the wheel. *Getting mad again won't solve the problem. If anything, your antagonism could make it worse.*

And *worse* might very well be a description of the current situation, given her tirade a few minutes ago, she granted, as she neared the harbor entrance and passed the diminutive Brant Point lighthouse adjacent to the Coast Guard station. Instead of reading him the riot act and following him like a persistent seagull follows a boat, she could have acquiesced to his explanation and headed home.

Yet what she'd told him had been true. She couldn't, in good conscience, leave anyone alone in the waters off Great Point. Even the disagreeable lieutenant. It was asking for trouble, no matter his skills or equipment. She'd dug in her heels for his own good, whether he appreciated it or not.

Not being the obvious conclusion. And that didn't bode well for a favorable response to her request—more like demand, she acceded—that he wipe the citation off her record.

The wharf came into sight, and Kate cut back the throttle, trying to recapture her earlier lighthearted mood. But that felt like ancient history now. As in B.C. Before Cole. And she doubted it would return unless the citation issue was resolved in her favor.

An outcome that seemed increasingly remote in light of their back-to-back unpleasant encounters.

With that conclusion, any lingering vestige of good cheer vanished as quickly as the sun in a sudden Nantucket storm.

Do you have a death wish or something?

Katherine MacDonald's question echoed again in Craig's mind as he jabbed at the buttons on his microwave. It had been bothering him since she'd voiced it six hours ago, and the refrain was beginning to get on his nerves.

Grabbing a soda out of the fridge, he pulled the tab, easing the pressure in the can with a pop and a fizz. Too bad it wasn't that easy to release the pressure inside of him, he lamented. Yet he couldn't lay the full blame for his tension on Ms. Mac-Donald. Although her blunt question had exacerbated it, in all honesty it had dogged him for three long years.

Exercise, he'd discovered, had proved to be a good temporary release valve. Ocean swimming in particular, especially when conditions were difficult. He'd never stopped to analyze why he sought out risky locations, but he supposed a psychologist delving into motivations might see it as a subconscious challenge to the sea: *You took my wife and son. Just try to take me.*

And there was some truth to that, he conceded. With every yard gained, with every swell overcome, with every undertow and riptide conquered, the pressure inside him dissipated. Each time he emerged whole and victorious from battling the waves, he felt a satisfying sense of triumph.

But the satisfaction didn't last long. And one of these days, if he continued to take chances, he'd lose. It was inevitable. In risky conditions, the odds were always stacked in favor of the sea. He knew that as well as the mouthy charter captain did.

And maybe that's what he wanted, deep inside, Craig was forced to admit. Maybe he wanted the sea to take him, too. To end the pain and loss and guilt forever. To give him the peace that had eluded him since the accident.

Katherine MacDonald might be right.

Maybe he did have a death wish.

The microwave pinged, and he withdrew the bland packaged dinner of sautéed chicken breast, broccoli and rice that had become one of his staples. He knew the drill by heart after three years of this fare: remove the plastic cover and let the meal rest until the steam escaped.

Rest.

The word stuck with him as he slid the disposable container onto the counter in the kitchen of the commander's quarters— a three-bedroom ranch house a mile from the station. Far enough removed to let the officer in charge find rest from his or her duties.

Unfortunately, the comfortable dwelling had the opposite effect on Craig. Though modest in size, the house felt cavernous and the silent rooms were depressing. Instead of being a haven of rest, it only served to remind him of all he'd lost.

As Craig straddled a stool at the counter and toyed with his meal, the passage from Matthew flashed through his mind: "Come to me, all you who labor and are burdened, and I will give you rest."

The minister had quoted those words at the funeral for his wife, Nicole, and his son, Aaron. But they'd been unable to penetrate his thick, isolating shroud of grief, offering no consolation then…or in the intervening years. All his life, he'd attended services every Sunday. But when tested by fire, he'd felt burned rather than fortified by the God he'd worshipped. Church attendance had become a meaningless gesture that left him feeling more empty and alone than if he hadn't gone. In time, he'd stopped the painful Sunday routine.

Routine.

Perhaps that was the key, Craig mused, dissecting a piece of broccoli with his fork. In many ways, his faith had become nothing more than a once-a-week visit to church, driven by habit rather than compelling belief. Perhaps if he approached services and prayer with an open heart, seeking God's will rather than demanding answers and immediate solace, the Lord would provide him with the peace and rest he craved.

It was worth a try, he supposed.

Because he couldn't keep living with the disheartening sense of hopelessness that plagued his days. Nor could he continue to take chances with his life, raising the stakes with every swimming excursion until at last he lost his gamble with the elements. It wasn't fair to Vicki. As Paul had reminded him, his daughter needed him. *Him.* Not the high-priced nannies he'd hired over the past three years, who saw to Vicki's physical needs but who couldn't give her the one thing she needed most.

A father's love.

Pushing aside his picked-over dinner, Craig rested his elbows on the counter and dropped his head into his hands as guilt gnawed at his gut, churning his dinner like an angry ocean agitates seaweed.

It wasn't Vicki's fault that she looked just like her mother, sharing the same blue-green eyes and hair the color of sun-ripened wheat. It wasn't her fault that every time he took her small hand he was reminded of the son he'd lost. And it wasn't her fault that he'd shut down emotionally to dull the pain, rendering him incapable of giving her the love she deserved—and needed.

As time passed, he'd known he had to make things right. The guilt over his neglect had begun to nag at him day and night, deepening the crushing burden of culpability he already carried. Although Vicki had never been a needy child, demanding attention or special care, she deserved the security of a loving parent. He hoped the move to Nantucket would give him the chance to provide that.

The rightness of his decision had been reinforced the day he'd left Vicki in his mother's care before heading to the island, with a promise to pick her up in six weeks, once he'd settled in.

As he'd knelt in front of her, prepared to give her a quick hug, she'd stopped him cold with a soft, uncertain question.

"Are you really coming back to get me?"

Jolted, he'd looked at her. Really looked—for the first time in a long while. And what he'd seen had made him want to cry.

Deep in those blue-green eyes had been a sadness and a loneliness as profound as his own. Far too profound for any child that age to know.

His had been caused by senseless deaths that had robbed his world of light and laughter.

But hers had been caused by him. The very man who should have loved her and protected her and made her world secure.

His throat constricting, he'd leaned over and pulled her close. "Yes, Vicki. I'm really coming back. And things will be different on Nantucket. I'm not going to work as much. We'll spend more time together."

When he'd released her, she'd stepped back and reached for his mother's hand, skepticism narrowing her eyes.

Truth be told, he shared her doubts. There was no manual, no rule book, no SOP for rebuilding a daughter's world and winning her love. He was flying by the seat of his pants, prepared to improvise as he went, as he'd often been called to do in precarious rescue situations.

He'd already decided there would be no more full-time nannies. He would only hand off her care while he was at work. For now, he'd lined up traditional day care, but in time he hoped to find a more personal, in-home arrangement.

He also planned to change his work habits. He'd put in a lot of hours these first few weeks on the job, learning the ropes, but once Vicki came he intended to leave work on time, pick her up at day care, fix dinner and spend the evening with her. And hope he could make up for all the years he'd abdicated his responsibilities.

Rising, Craig deposited his half-eaten dinner in the trash, reminding himself to stock up on some kid-friendly food before he picked her up in two weeks. And he needed to prepare a room for her. A place where she would feel welcome and loved.

He also needed to get over the death wish a certain outspoken charter-fishing boat captain had forced him to confront.

Craig swiped at a few stray crumbs on the counter, leaving the surface pristine, as he thought back over his encounters with the red-haired dynamo. Although he might not appreciate being on the receiving end of Katherine MacDonald's fiery temper, he had to give credit where it was due.

She wasn't easily intimidated. And she said what she thought. Like it or not.

To his surprise, Craig found his lips curving into a smile as he pictured her on the deck of the *Lucy Sue,* eyes blazing, cheeks aflame, hair whipped by the wind as she'd glared at him. And while he finished tidying up the kitchen and prepared to call it a day, he found himself looking forward to their next encounter.

Which made no sense at all.

Chapter Three

"I have to run a couple of errands, Barlow. I'll be back in an hour."

Ben looked up from his desk and grinned at the commander, who was standing in the doorway. "No problem. I've got it covered."

"There's not much to cover. It's a pretty quiet Monday."

"Enjoy it while it lasts. Once the day-trippers and summer people arrive, you won't have a minute to call your own. You won't believe some of the calls we get. Last year, some guy forgot to install his drain plug and ended up sinking his boat."

A smile tugged at Craig's lips. "I can't wait."

"Trust me. You can."

His smile lingering, Craig took advantage of the springlike weather and headed down Easton Street on foot. From what he'd gleaned about his predecessor, Sandra Medart had had a high profile on the island. Most Nantucketers had known her on sight, and both locals and crew had liked and respected her. She'd initiated a popular boating safety program, attended all community events and maintained an open-door policy, encouraging anyone with marine-based concerns to come directly to her. According to Barlow, she'd excelled at the PR aspect of the job.

To date, he'd done little to emulate her example. Now that he had his sea legs, however, he figured it was time to show his face in the community. And a walk through town wouldn't be a bad place to start.

Turning onto South Beach Street, it took him mere minutes to reach the heart of the historic town, with its cobblestone streets and labyrinth of tiny lanes. He knew his dark blue slacks and matching shirt, with the twin silver bars on the collar that signaled his rank, would identify him at a glance as the new commander, and as he strolled around he drew more than a few curious looks. Only year-rounders populated the quiet town center on this early April Monday, and when he nodded and smiled in response to their discreet perusal, several approached to welcome him.

Forty-five minutes later, after grabbing a paper at The Hub and stopping at a few other spots Barlow had identified as local hangouts, he headed down Main Street toward the harbor. After three short blocks, the cobblestones of the town's primary thoroughfare merged with Straight Wharf, where many of the commercial boats were docked.

The *Lucy Sue* among them.

Pausing at the entrance to the wharf, Craig debated his next move. As he'd left the station, he'd tucked the original copy of Katherine MacDonald's citation in his pocket. But the matter didn't require his personal attention; he could send one of his crew members later to handle the resolution of such a minor violation.

Except it wasn't minor to Ms. MacDonald. She'd made that very clear. And as long as he was in the area, he supposed he ought to stop by and see if he could smooth things out—all in the interest of good PR, of course. Why else would he put himself in the path of the human hurricane?

A few reasons popped to mind, but he quickly squelched them. Despite appealing green eyes that flashed with life and passion, despite the intriguing juxtaposition of a delicate physical appearance with a strong character, despite vibrant hair that sparked with every movement, only a masochist would want to deal with her temper.

He was here on business. Period.

His decision made, Craig strode past the shuttered souvenir shops. Within minutes he found the *Lucy Sue,* gently rocking in her slip on the wharf. There was no sign of the red-haired skipper—or anyone else. No surprise there, he supposed, considering most owners wintered their boats on the mainland. Those who didn't spent little time aboard in the off season.

What did surprise him was the flutter of disappointment in the pit of his stomach. Where in the world had that come from? Last night he'd found himself looking forward to their next encounter, and today he was seeking her out. Logic told him he should be going out of his way to avoid another exchange with the argumentative captain.

But for some reason he wasn't.

Rather than try to analyze his odd reaction, he propped his fists on his hips and surveyed the boat at close range. He knew from the citation that the *Lucy Sue* was an older model, but he hadn't realized how old. She had to have been built twenty or twenty-five years ago, he estimated. Yet she was well maintained. He saw no evidence of barnacles below the water line, nor any indication of oxidation topside, suggesting the fiberglass hull was polished and waxed on a regular basis. The deck was stain-free, and the teak trim had been varnished rather than allowed to weather to whitish-gray. The finish looked fresh, too, free of obvious chips or scuffs. It was clear a lot of elbow grease had gone into keeping the boat in tip-top condition.

While everything he could see was cosmetic, Craig knew that anyone who took such meticulous care of the appearance of a boat was likely to be as diligent about mechanical maintenance—and safety. In light of the number of charter slips, he also concluded that Ms. MacDonald hadn't been exaggerating about the competition. Two good reasons why the flare citation had upset her.

And based on the traces of worry and sorrow he'd glimpsed in her eyes as she'd squared off with him across his desk on Friday, the last thing she needed in her life was more stress.

Craig couldn't erase the events that had led to that emotional confrontation. But if she'd followed through and replaced the flares, as she'd promised, disposing of the citation in his pocket was going to be his top priority this afternoon.

What was the Coast Guard commander doing at the *Lucy Sue?*

Kate's step faltered as she turned a corner on Straight Wharf and caught sight of the tall officer standing beside her boat. The last thing she wanted was another skirmish with the line-toeing lieutenant.

For a few heartbeats she considered retreating. His back was to her, giving her a good view of his broad shoulders as he looked over the *Lucy Sue.* She could disappear before he noticed her.

But running from problems didn't solve them. If he'd decided to let the citation stand, she might as well get the bad news now rather than later. And his presence suggested the news was bad rather than good. Why else would he come in person, except to turn the tables and wield his authority by scuttling her request? After the way she'd treated him in their previous encounters, she couldn't blame him if he took advantage of the opportunity to put her in her place.

Her shoulders slumped a fraction, and she shifted the bag she was toting from one arm to the other. Then she forced her feet to carry her forward, her sport shoes noiseless on the wharf. She stopped a few feet away from the grim reaper and drew a fortifying breath.

"Planning to do another inspection, Lieutenant?" She'd intended to keep her tone neutral, but a touch of defiance crept in.

He swung toward her, his features etched with surprise. And some other emotion she couldn't identify.

"That wasn't on my agenda."

"Following up on the one already done, then."

"Yes. I was in town anyway and thought I'd drop by."

"I got the flares." She edged passed him on the finger pier, juggling the bag as she prepared to board.

"Let me hold that for you." He took the sack from her before she could protest, glancing at the package of spark plugs on top. "Engine problems?"

Rather than give him a direct answer, she swung into the boat and reached for the bag. "I'm always prepared."

"You do your own maintenance?"

"Most of it. My neighbor helps me on the trickier things. And speaking of being prepared, let me show you the new flares." She ducked into the cabin, retrieved the flares and rejoined him thirty seconds later on the wharf. "As you'll see, I'm covered for the new season." She handed them over, annoyed once again at the defensive note that had crept into her voice. For the life of her she couldn't manage a pleasant tone with this man.

The lieutenant took the flares in silence, scanned the expiration dates and handed them back. "Everything seems to be in order."

Tipping his head, he folded his arms across his chest. His powerful, well-developed chest, Kate couldn't help noticing, her gaze dropping in the direction of the name tag on his shirt pocket.

"So what happens next?" She forced her chin back up,

toward eyes as blue as the ocean on a sunny Nantucket summer day. Tensing, she braced for bad news.

He reached into the pocket of his slacks and withdrew the original citation, which had been folded into neat, precise squares. Watching her, he tore it into small pieces, disposing of them in a trash can a few steps away.

Her eyes widened. "Does that mean…are you going to expunge it from my record?"

"Yes."

"Why?"

"Your request was reasonable. Even if you weren't." He gave her an assessing look, a touch of amusement sparking in his irises. "Do you always overreact when you're angry?"

It was a fair, but incendiary, question, and she stiffened. "I've been told I don't suffer fools gladly."

He cocked one eyebrow but remained silent.

You idiot! Kate chided herself, hot color stealing onto her cheeks. *The man has just done you a huge favor, and you insult him instead of thanking him? How ungracious is that?*

Swallowing past her embarrassment, Kate shoved her hands into the front pockets of her jeans. "Look, can we start over?"

"That might not be a bad idea."

"Okay. Good. The thing is, I appreciate your consideration. I'm sure you noticed the *Lucy Sue* is an older model. It's not as jazzy as most of the other charter boats, nor does it have all the bells and whistles. A clean safety record is a selling point I can use in my advertising to help me compete. Without it…" She shook her head and shrugged.

"My executive petty officer tells me you've been at this a while, Ms. MacDonald."

The wind whipped a lock of hair across her cheek, and she tucked it behind her ear. "Yes. My father-in-law started the business. He retired and passed it on to me and my husband when we married. But I've been fishing my whole life." She moistened her lips as she considered whether to extend an olive branch, then decided it couldn't hurt. "By the way, my friends call me Kate."

She noted the flicker of surprise in his eyes, as well as the twitch that tugged at the corner of his mouth. "As in *Kiss Me, Kate?*"

At the mention of the Cole Porter musical based on Shakespeare's *Taming of the Shrew*, Kate grimaced. "I suppose that's a fair question in light of our relationship to date. And I apologize for my bad temper. You hit me on a rough couple of days. Believe it or not, despite my red hair I usually stay on a pretty even keel."

The skeptical tilt of his head brought a rueful smile to her lips.

"I don't blame you for doubting that claim. But it's true, Lieutenant."

He returned her smile. "The name is Craig. And I suppose I'll find out the truth for myself if our paths cross again."

"I expect they will on occasion. It's not a very big island. Unless you continue to be the invisible man."

A puzzled frown creased his brow. "The what?"

Grinning, she shoved her hands deeper into the pockets of her jeans. "The invisible man. That's what the locals are calling you. You've hardly shown your face in public."

"I've been busy getting up to speed at the station. But I'll be more visible in the community in the future."

"I'm sure everyone will look forward to that."

He shot her a speculative glance, as if he was tempted to ask whether she looked forward to it, too. Instead, he smiled and edged back. "In the meantime, a pile of paperwork awaits me."

"Thank you again for your help with the citation."

"It was my pleasure, Kate. Take care." With a wave, he headed toward Main Street.

She watched him leave, liking the sound of her name on

his lips, waiting until he disappeared before boarding the *Lucy Sue* to tackle her chores.

But long after he was gone, she kept replaying their conversation in her mind. For once, it had not only been civil, but enjoyable. And he'd proved to be more flexible than she'd anticipated, bending the rules for her despite the way she'd treated him. In his place, she doubted she would have been so forgiving—or generous.

As she stored her supplies below, Kate was forced to concede that her initial assessment of the commander as a stuffy, rigid, rule follower might have been a little too hasty—and a little too harsh. Still, one cordial exchange wasn't enough to convince her she'd been entirely wrong about his character. Before she revised her opinion, she'd have to see a whole lot more of him.

And much to her surprise, despite their rocky start and her earlier resolve to avoid him as much as possible, she found that prospect quite appealing.

"I smell cinnamon! Oh, goodie!"

Breaking free of Kate's grasp, Maddie headed straight for the plate of cinnamon toast waiting for her on the hickory table in Edith's cozy kitchen, her eyes bright with pleasure.

"I gave her breakfast already, Edith. You didn't have to do that." Kate entered her neighbor's back door at a more sedate pace, stopping two steps into the room.

"I wanted to. I like doing things for people I care about. Have some coffee."

"I can't. I'm already running late."

"You can be at the high school in five minutes. I'll pour you a cup to go." Edith retrieved an insulated mug with a lid from the cabinet and lifted the pot from the coffeemaker. "Besides, I wanted to tell you about an interesting experience I had last night."

The woman's studied casualness put Kate on alert. "What happened?"

"I met your lieutenant at the market." She added cream to Kate's coffee with a quick tip of the pitcher. "I must admit, his manner wasn't at all what I anticipated based on your description. He was charming."

Kate's neck grew warm. "I've revised my opinion a bit."

"Since when?"

"Since he erased the citation from my record yesterday."

"Did he, now? How interesting." The older woman secured the lid on the mug and grinned at Kate. "Must have been your charm."

Kate made a face at her. "Very funny." Checking her watch, she hoisted her purse higher on her shoulder and changed the subject. "I've got to run, Edith. It sets a very bad example when the teachers are tardy. Call me if you have any problems with Maddie."

"I've got the nebulizer routine down if we need it. Don't worry."

A shadow of distress tightened Kate's features. "It's hard not to."

"You know what Mac would have said."

"Yes." The whisper of a smile tugged at the corners of her mouth. "'Don't look for trouble.'" She leaned over and hugged the gray-haired woman, who was more like family than mere neighbor or friend. "I'm sorry I've had to call on you so often this school year. I can't remember ever being asked to sub this much. But the extra money's been a godsend."

Edith waved the comment aside. "I don't mind in the least. Maddie's a charmer. And speaking of charmers—the lieutenant fits that definition in my book."

Once Edith sank her teeth into a topic, she was as hard to shake loose as the island's notorious deer ticks, Kate reflected.

"Like I said, he's not as bad as I first thought." She reached for the doorknob.

"He doesn't think you're too bad, either, despite your show of temper."

Kate swung back. "He talked about me?"

"Only after I happened to mention we were neighbors."

Edith's innocent expression didn't fool Kate. There was no *happen to* about it. When the Lighthouse Lane matron was on a mission, she could be as single-minded as a Nantucket whaler of old in hot pursuit of his quarry. Kate clutched her purse strap as her pulse accelerated. "You didn't tell him what I said about him, did you?"

"Of course not." Edith sniffed and gave her an indignant look. "That was between the two of us. I merely mentioned I'd known you for years and that you were a wonderful person—and a hard worker. He said he'd been impressed by your determination and complimented the *Lucy Sue*. Called her a fine boat, and said you'd taken great care of her."

"What else did you two talk about?"

"Nothing." The corners of Edith's mouth turned down in disgust. "His cell phone rang just as the conversation was getting interesting. Some emergency at the station."

Expelling a relieved breath, Kate once more hitched her purse into position. "I'll be back around three-thirty."

"Bye, Mommy." Maddie waved and took another huge bite of cinnamon toast.

Smiling, Kate moved beside her daughter to place a quick peck on her cheek. "Be good for Mrs. Shaw, okay?"

"Okay."

"See you later, Edith." With a wave, Kate let herself out.

For the next five minutes, as she navigated the maze of narrow streets that led to the school, Kate considered Edith's chance encounter with the lieutenant. Thank goodness his cell phone had interrupted their conversation, or Edith would have told the commander her neighbor's life story. The embellished version, Kate suspected.

As it was, Edith had only managed to get in a brief complimentary remark. To which the lieutenant has responded that he'd admired Kate's determination.

Determination. That was a generous way to describe her approach in their first two altercations, she supposed, considering hostility and rudeness might be more accurate. She should be grateful for his diplomacy.

Yet she found herself wishing he'd been able to find some other quality to admire. Intelligence, strength, vivaciousness, competence…it would have been nice if he'd noticed one of those attributes.

Shaking her head, Kate chided herself for her silly waste of brain power. The lieutenant had wiped her record clean. That was the important thing. It shouldn't matter what he thought about her.

Yet, much to her annoyance, it did.

Chapter Four

"Well, my stars, look who's here!"

At Edith's whispered comment, Kate followed her line of sight as they walked down the church aisle on Sunday.

Seated in a pew halfway down on the left was none other than Lieutenant Craig Cole. She could only see his back, but there was no mistaking that dark blond hair or those broad shoulders.

Grabbing her neighbor's arm, Kate indicated a pew beside her. "This is fine."

The older woman kept moving, dragging Kate along with her. "We never sit this far back."

"Edith." Kate hissed the name, and the older woman paused. "Maddie and I are going to sit here today."

After a brief hesitation, Edith shrugged. "Suit yourself." She tucked her arm through Chester's. "We'll see you afterward."

She headed straight for the pew behind the commander.

"Mommy, how come we aren't sitting with Mr. and Mrs. Shaw?"

Maddie's childish, high-pitched voice carried throughout the house of worship, and Kate shushed her, dipping her head as she ushered her daughter into the pew. Though she kept her face averted, she couldn't hide her red hair. If the lieutenant turned around, he'd spot her immediately.

"I thought it might be nice to sit somewhere different today." She pitched her voice low, hoping her daughter would take the hint.

No such luck. Maddie's version of whispering was to lean close while speaking in a normal tone. "But I can't see the front. We're too far back."

In general, Kate didn't believe bribery should be used to control a child's behavior. Today she made an exception.

"Maddie, honey, it's just for this one week. And if you're very good and stay very quiet, I'll take you to Downyflake afterward."

The promise of a visit to the well-loved doughnut establishment did the trick. There wasn't a peep out of Maddie for the rest of the service. She folded her hands in her lap, sang along with the hymns she knew and kept her attention fixed on the sanctuary. She was the picture of piousness.

In contrast, Kate fidgeted throughout the entire service. She crossed and uncrossed her legs, trying to find a comfortable position. She wandered off the melody of a familiar hymn, arching the eyebrows of a few nearby congregants. She couldn't concentrate on Reverend Kaizer's sermon.

All thanks to a certain Coast Guard commander sitting a dozen rows away.

It was ridiculous.

But there wasn't a thing she could do about it.

In the end, she stopped trying to ignore him and allowed herself a few discreet peeks in his direction. He'd ditched his uniform, she noted. Dressed in civilian clothes, he projected a far different aura than when on the job. Less authoritarian. Less severe. More human—and approachable. And the man had good taste. His dark gray slacks, white shirt and charcoal tweed jacket conveyed a quiet, casual elegance that suited his lean, muscular frame.

As the organ struck up the final hymn, Kate helped Maddie on with her coat. Thank goodness they'd driven themselves to church instead of hitching a ride with Edith and Chester, as usual. That meant they could escape quickly.

The instant the last note of the final hymn died away, she hustled Maddie out the door and toward the car, exchanging greetings with members of the congregation without slowing her pace. Only after they pulled out of their parking place and were on their way toward the south end of town did her respiration return to normal.

They were safe.

Safe.

What an odd choice of words, Kate thought, as she swung into the last parking space in Downyflake's lot and she and Maddie joined the long line that spilled out the front door. Why didn't she feel safe around the new commander? And why had she felt the need to escape from him?

It had nothing to do with his position of authority, that much she knew. While she'd been upset by the citation, she'd felt angry, not threatened. Nor had she felt in the least intimidated—or unsafe—when she'd marched over to his office and laid into him about it or when she'd rebuked him for taking chances off Great Point. The unsafe feeling was more…personal…than that.

And it didn't take her long to pinpoint its origins: the moment in his office when he'd looked into her eyes and tapped into her private sorrows and deepest insecurities. While he might not know what they were, he knew they were there.

Unsettling as that had been, Kate wasn't concerned about the commander using that insight against her. She sensed he had too much integrity and honor for that. So the mere fact he'd breached her defenses, albeit disconcerting, wasn't what made her feel vulnerable.

Then what did?

The line inched forward as she pondered that question. And when the answer came, it took her breath away.

She felt unsafe—and in need of escape—because, for the first time since she'd lost Mac, she was attracted to a man.

"Mommy, you're hurting my hand!"

At Maddie's protest, Kate immediately loosened her grip and bent to give the youngster a hug. "I'm sorry, honey. We're almost to the counter." Her words came out choppy as she struggled to slow her staccato pulse. "What kind of doughnut are you going to get?"

"Sugar."

"How come I knew that?" It took every ounce of her will-power to adopt a teasing tone and summon up the semblance of a normal smile. Especially when thoughts of the commander's deep blue eyes, athletic build and aura of steadiness and strength left her feeling anything but normal.

No question about it. That little flutter in her stomach was attraction.

And it scared her silly.

Because no matter what Edith thought—she wasn't ready for another romance. Besides, the lieutenant wasn't her type. He was the exact opposite of Mac, who'd brightened her days with his agreeable, relaxed attitude and easygoing charm. Who'd seen life through a lens that captured nuances of color and texture rather than mere black and white.

While Kate couldn't deny the odd magnetic pull she felt toward the new Coast Guard commander, it had to be an anomaly. Perhaps induced by the power of Edith's suggestion, she speculated. Or maybe it was the result of the deep-seated loneliness that, to her surprise, had intensified rather than dissipated since Mac's death. Plus, Lieutenant Cole had caught her at a vulnerable time, thanks to her shaky finances and concerns about Maddie. Anyone in her situation would be susceptible to the competence he radiated and attracted by the broad shoulders that looked capable of carrying the heaviest load.

His empathetic blue eyes had nothing at all to do with it.

That was her story, she decided, as she stepped up to the counter at Downyflake.

And she was sticking to it.

As Craig slid behind the wheel of his late-model Camry, he surveyed the modest church. A few people remained near the front door, but most had departed after exchanging a few words with him. It had been a good morning, both from a spiritual and PR perspective. He'd taken a first step in reconnecting with the Lord, and he'd met quite a few of the locals.

Edith Shaw, Kate's neighbor, had been there, too. According to the older woman, who'd managed to ferret quite a bit of information out of him during their short walk to the back of church after the service, Kate had also attended. But by the time they'd emerged onto the small lawn, she'd disappeared.

He couldn't help wondering if his presence had prompted the charter captain's evasive maneuver.

Guiding his car through the town's narrow streets, he headed for the small bakery/restaurant across from the market. As Barlow had promised, the food was good, the prices reasonable. An exception on an island where he'd discovered most prices weren't. The high cost of living on Nantucket had been a shocker.

As he approached his destination, the packed lot and the throng at the door almost dissuaded him. But a car backing out of a spot at the far end of the lot clinched his decision. Swinging into the parking area, he made a beeline for it.

The man behind the wheel of the departing car grinned and gave him a thumbs-up as he passed, and Craig waved in return. Claiming the spot, he set the brake and prepared to enjoy a rare high-fat, high-carb breakfast.

As he exited the car, he turned toward the restaurant—and came face-to-face with the red-haired captain on the other side of the adjacent car.

Her eyes widened and a flush rose on her cheeks, giving him the answer to his earlier question.

She'd bolted from the church because she'd wanted to avoid him.

And she'd do it again if she could, he suspected. But there was no polite way to sidestep conversation with only the roof of a car separating them.

"Good morning, Kate."

"Lieutenant."

He dug deep for his most charming smile. The one he hadn't used in years. It felt stiff and rusty, like the hinges on a long unopened gate. "I thought we'd moved past the formalities."

"Sorry."

He waited, but when she didn't say anything else, he pocketed his keys and nodded toward the restaurant. "Indulging in a few treats?"

"Yes."

For a woman who'd had no trouble spewing out plenty of words in their previous encounters, her reticence bordered on alarming. "Is everything okay?"

She blushed. "Fine."

He tried a different tack. "I thought the sermon was excellent, didn't you?"

Her face went blank. Then the flush of color on her cheeks deepened. "Yes."

"Mommy, who is that man?"

The childish voice took Craig off guard, and he shifted to better see through the windows of Kate's car. A little girl with long, raven-colored hair stared back at him through the glass, her expression curious, her dark eyes big in a face that seemed a little too pale. He estimated her age at four or five.

The same as Vicki's.

The child's question loosened Kate's vocal chords. "That's the new lieutenant from the Coast Guard station, honey."

"You mean the invisible man?"

Sending Craig a sheepish glance, she responded to her daughter. "He's not invisible anymore, though, is he?"

"I bet he was just too busy to come out before, like I said. Weren't you?" The last part was addressed to him.

"That's right." He moved out from between the cars and stepped around the back of Kate's older-model Honda. The little girl was dressed in a plaid jumper with a red turtleneck sweater underneath, white tights and shiny black shoes. Her hair was pulled back with a red ribbon, though a few wisps had escaped to form soft waves around her face. She was charming.

But no more so than her mother, Craig decided. Today Kate had traded her work-worn jeans, slicker and T-shirt for a slim black skirt, black pumps and a long-sleeved green angora sweater the color of her eyes. Her hair had been tamed with barrettes on each side of a center part and lay soft on her shoulders. A touch of lipstick drew his attention to her mouth, and his pulse took a leap.

Needing a distraction, he crouched down and smiled at the little girl. "My name's Craig. What's yours?"

"My real name is Madison, but everybody calls me Maddie."

"That's a very pretty name."

"Thank you." She gave him a shy smile and dipped her head.

"Looks like you're taking some treats home." He tapped the white bag clutched in her hand.

"I ate one doughnut here. We sat on the bench over there so we wouldn't spill milk in the car or get sugar on the seats." She pointed across the parking lot toward the front door. "Mommy said I can eat the other one at home. Are you going to get a doughnut?"

"I might."

She leaned closer, her demeanor serious. "The sugar ones are best," she confided.

"I'll keep that in mind."

Standing, Craig found Kate rummaging through her purse.

"I must have left my keys inside. Or on the bench." Giving up the search, she shook her head and inspected the shoulder-to-shoulder crowd in dismay. "I guess we'll have to go back in."

"Maddie and I could wait here, if you'd like. It might be easier to get through the mob alone."

Her hesitation didn't surprise him. He might be in a high-profile position, but they were barely acquainted—and the news was filled with horror stories about crimes against children.

Propping a hip on the back of her car, he let his fingers curve around the edge of the trunk. "You could see us the whole time, Kate. We'll stay right here."

He hadn't expected his follow-up to come out in such a gentle, understanding tone. The subtle arch of her eyebrows told him she hadn't, either. But it did the trick.

"Thanks. I'll be back in three minutes." She touched Maddie on the shoulder, the simple gold band on her left hand flashing in the sunlight. "Stay here with the lieutenant, okay, honey?"

"Okay."

With one more quick look in his direction, Kate strode back toward the restaurant.

As she plunged into the horde, Craig thought about her ring. He'd noticed it in his office, too. Why wasn't her husband with her today? he wondered. Perhaps he wasn't a man of faith. Or they might be divorced.

His curiosity piqued, Craig considered the best way to satisfy it. He couldn't very well broach the subject of her marital status with Kate. She'd think it odd, inappropriate and irrelevant. And it was. Yet he wanted to know.

He looked down at Maddie. She stood quietly beside him,

her fingers crimped around the top of the white bag. Feeling like a heel for the strategy that popped into his mind, he nevertheless dropped down to her level again.

"Do you come to Downyflake for doughnuts every Sunday, Maddie?"

"No. Just sometimes. I wish we could come every day, though. It's my favoritist place."

Chuckling, Craig rested his forearms on this thighs, noting again the little girl's pallor. Did she have health issues? Was that another reason for the anxiety in Kate's eyes?

But that would have to be a question for another day. He only had three minutes, and they were ticking by fast.

"When I was little, there was an ice cream shop not too far from where I lived. That was my favorite place. In the summer, my daddy would take me and my mommy there after dinner. Like you come here."

Maddie's expression grew wistful. "I don't have a daddy. He died before I was borned."

Stunned, Craig tried to process this new information. Kate was a widow. Had become one while pregnant with her husband's child.

When the silence lengthened, Maddie hit him with a question of her own. "Do you have any little boys or girls, Lootenin?"

As he struggled to come up with a response to the unexpected—and disconcerting—query, Kate reappeared.

"I found them." She jingled the keys and opened the back door. "In you go, honey." She hustled the little girl into her car seat, secured the straps and shut the door.

Craig saw the apology in her eyes when she turned to him, telling him she'd overheard her daughter's question. "I'm afraid Maddie has a tendency to give people the third degree. And she seems to have inherited her mother's bluntness. I'm hoping it gives way to tact and discretion as she ages—unlike her mother's."

At her self-deprecating humor Craig dredged up a fleeting grin. "I think maybe I just caught her mother on a couple of bad days."

"Thanks for cutting me some slack."

"I'm guessing you deserve it."

Why he'd said that, Craig had no idea. It was obvious Kate didn't, either. She edged away, her knuckles white on her purse strap.

"Thanks for watching Maddie." A slight tremor ran through her voice.

"My pleasure." His response came out husky, and he cleared his throat. "I'm glad you found your keys."

The words were innocuous. But the sudden sizzle of electricity between them wasn't.

Fumbling for the car door, Kate slid in and pulled it shut. He stepped aside. She backed out. He headed for the restaurant.

End of story.

Except for one thing.

His heart wouldn't stop pounding.

Blown away by the unexpected reaction, he looked back toward the parking lot as he reached the door. He caught Kate watching him instead of the traffic on the road. Although she yanked her gaze away at once, he'd seen enough to know that Kate MacDonald had been as stunned as he'd been by that electric moment.

And he was equally certain that, like him, she was determined to ignore it.

"How's it coming, Chester?"

As Kate and Maddie stepped through the gate in the tall privet hedge that separated her tiny back lawn from her neighbor's more spacious grounds, Chester set aside his paintbrush.

"Hi, Kate. Good afternoon, Miss Maddie." He tipped an

imaginary hat to the little girl, eliciting a giggle. "It's coming. A few more nice days like this, I'll wrap it up."

"I wouldn't count on the good weather lasting if I were you."

"We can hope, though, can't we?"

Kate had read somewhere once that a lot of Nantucketers spend the winter waiting for the summer. She wasn't one of them. Like Mac had, she loved Nantucket in all her guises. But Edith and Chester had only lived here ten years, moving to the island after Chester retired. They hadn't yet grown accustomed to Nantucket's long winters.

"Yes, we can. It's looking good." Kate scanned the small outbuilding Chester was renovating into an efficiency cottage to rent to summer people. When he'd come up with the idea two years ago, Edith had endorsed it wholeheartedly, excited about the extra source of income. Her enthusiasm had waned, however, as Chester became distracted with other projects and the remodeling dragged on.

How the two of them had ever gotten together was a mystery to Kate. Chester was patient and slow-moving, while Edith bustled about, bristling with energy. Yet they seemed to complement one another, accepting their differences with indulgent affection. And their shared love of Nantucket was deep. They were active in multiple island organizations and causes, and Edith was one of the most connected people Kate knew.

She was also one of the main branches of the very active local grapevine. There was no better source of island news than Edith Shaw. And Kate suspected that was the reason for the summons that had been waiting on her answering machine when she and Maddie returned from an emergency run to the grocery store after she'd discovered the gallon of milk she'd bought a few days ago had soured.

Wiping his hands on a paint-smeared rag, Chester examined his handiwork, a shock of gray hair falling over his forehead. "It'll be a fine little hideaway. Good for honeymooners who want lots of privacy." He grinned and gave Kate a wink. "I know Edith doesn't believe it'll be ready this season, but I'm determined to finish it up. How's the *Lucy Sue* running?"

"So far, so good."

"You let me know if she needs any more adjustments."

"What would I do without you?" She leaned over and gave him a quick hug.

He flushed and shoved his fingers through his hair, wreaking havoc with the ornery cowlick no amount of hair gel could subdue. "You could turn a man's head with that kind of talk." Grinning, he tipped his head toward the house. "Edith call you over?"

"Mmm-hmm. Said she had a loaf of homemade pumpkin bread with my name on it."

He chuckled. They both knew Edith always offered a treat when she had news to impart or wanted a gab fest. "That's what I figured. You go on in. She's probably chomping at the bit. As for you, Miss Maddie, I know an old man who could use a helper for a few minutes."

Puzzled, the little girl looked around the yard. "Where is he?"

Chester grinned. "Takes after her mother in the flattery department, I see. You're going to have to watch her with the gentlemen when she gets older." He winked at Kate again and took Maddie's hand. "So you don't think I'm old, hmm?"

As he led her daughter toward a toolbox on the other side of the small cottage, Kate crossed the yard and knocked on Edith's back door. Within seconds it was pulled open.

"What's this about pumpkin bread?" Kate stepped across the threshold and sniffed. The air was redolent with the aroma of cinnamon and cloves. "Mmm…it smells good in here."

"My sentiments exactly."

Checking behind the door for the source of the comment, Kate smiled at Heather Anderson, her neighbor on the other side. With her light brown hair touched with gold, statuesque height and graceful carriage, she had the perfect demeanor for her chosen profession—running The Devon Rose tearoom on the first floor of her spacious house. Though the two women's different work schedules didn't allow much opportunity for interaction, they shared a mutual liking and respect.

"Taking the day off?" Kate asked her.

"I wish. I have a full house for afternoon tea. I just stopped over to return Edith's rolling pin. Mine broke in the middle of making scones. See you two later." She exited with a wave.

As the door closed behind her, Edith turned to Kate. "I have some news."

Chester had been right, Kate thought in amusement. Edith was bursting to share whatever tidbit she'd picked up. But she kept her smile in check as she teased the older woman. "I know. I got the message about the pumpkin bread."

"Pumpkin bread?" Edith's face went blank. "Oh, yes. The pumpkin bread. It's all wrapped and waiting for you." She gestured vaguely toward the counter. "This is more important than that. Guess who I ran into at Bartlett's Farm a little while ago?"

Considering that many of the islanders visited the upscale market and garden center on a regular basis, Kate was clueless. "I have no idea."

"Lieutenant Cole." Edith beamed at her.

Her matchmaking neighbor had a one-track mind, Kate concluded, determined to cut the conversation short as she sidled over to the counter to retrieve the pumpkin bread.

"That's nice." She picked up the bread and edged toward the door.

"Wait. There's more. He's available."

Kate reached for the knob. "For what?"

"You know perfectly well what I mean, Katherine Mac-Donald." Edith shot her a disgruntled look. "He's not attached. The poor man lost his wife several years ago."

Kate dropped her hand. "He's a widower?"

"Yes. With a daughter. A four-year-old named Vicki."

Edith had reeled her in hook, line and sinker, Kate granted, taking a step back into the room. "She wasn't at church with him this morning."

"That's because she's staying with his mother in Wisconsin while he settles in. Here's the thing, Kate. When I mentioned that I watch Maddie for you, he asked if I'd be willing to take Vicki, too. He's got day care set up but would rather have her in a more personal setting. I told him I'd be happy to, but that it was really your decision, since I committed to you first. And it might not be a bad thing for Maddie to have some companionship under the age of sixty. She spends way too much time with me and Chester."

Edith fished in the pocket of her skirt, pulled out a slip of paper and handed it over. "That's the lieutenant's phone number. I told him I'd ask you to call him tonight so the two of you could discuss this."

Taking the paper, Kate frowned. "I don't know, Edith. Are you sure you're up to two four-year-olds?"

The woman dismissed the comment with a wave. "I like having children around. Besides, I suspect having two little ones will end up being less work for me. They can entertain each other."

Her neighbor's rationale was logical, Kate conceded. And it would be nice for Maddie to have a child her own age to play with. No other children lived on Lighthouse Lane, and her daughter's asthma problem had kept her more confined than most youngsters her age.

"Okay, Edith. I'll give him a call."

"Good. Worst case, we give it a try and it doesn't work. But I have a feeling everyone will benefit from this arrangement."

Kate didn't like the twinkle in her neighbor's eye. "How so?"

"Maybe Maddie and Vicki won't be the only two to pair up."

"Edith." Kate shoved her hair back, exasperated. She was beginning to think nothing was going to dissuade the woman from her newfound quest to find a suitable match for her. "Leave me out of the equation, okay? If you're so bent on matchmaking, why don't you push him in Heather's direction? She's single." Kate eased the door open.

"He's not the right man for her. Besides, she has no interest in romance."

"Neither do I."

"Baloney."

Kate did a double take. "What's that supposed to mean?"

"Baloney. As in hogwash. My dear girl, you're a young and vibrant woman. You've mourned for four long years. You can't tell me you're not as lonely as that lieutenant has to be."

Her neighbor knew her too well, Kate lamented. It was useless to pretend. "I miss Mac, Edith. And yes, I get lonely. But one romance was enough. Mac was the only man for me." She hefted the pumpkin loaf on her palm and managed the semblance of a smile as she took one step out the door. "Thanks again for this. Maddie and I will enjoy it." Without waiting for a response, Kate slipped out.

But as she collected her daughter and they headed home, Kate mulled over what Edith had said. Craig Cole might very well be lonely. Yet if he'd suffered a loss, as she had, he might be as reluctant to consider romance as she was. There was a huge chasm between available and amenable.

And Kate had a strong suspicion that while she and the lieutenant both fell into the available camp, neither of them was anywhere close to making the leap to amenable.

Chapter Five

She was five minutes late.

Craig shifted in his seat at the small table in the café on Main Street, taking a sip of coffee while watching the front door. Kate hadn't sounded all that eager about meeting him for lunch when she'd called last night to discuss his day-care proposal, suggesting they talk on the phone instead. But after he'd told her there was more to the story than appeared on the surface, she relented and had promised to meet him on his lunch hour.

After another five minutes passed, however, he began to wonder if she'd changed her mind. Although Edith had appeared agreeable to his proposal, perhaps Kate preferred to maintain the status quo so her daughter had the older woman's undivided attention. He couldn't blame her for that. But for Vicki's sake he'd hoped—

The front door jangled and to his relief Kate stepped over the threshold. But not the Kate he'd expected. Instead of her customary weekday attire of jeans and a slicker, she wore black slacks, a green turtleneck sweater and a black wool coat. And she seemed a little harried.

Standing, Craig waved at her, and she headed in his direction. Another patron hailed her en route, however, and she stopped to exchange a few words. By the time she arrived at his table, she was breathless and apologetic.

"Sorry. I got delayed at school." She slipped into the chair he held, shrugging out of her coat as she spoke.

"School?" He retook his seat.

"I sub at the high school. English, mostly."

"I thought you ran a charter business."

"I do. In season. In the off season, I'm a substitute teacher. In case you haven't noticed, the cost of living on the island is high. It's tough to make ends meet with just seasonal work."

The waiter appeared as Craig digested this new piece of information. Kate had two jobs. No wonder she often looked tired. And stressed.

After Kate ordered a bowl of quahog chowder and he opted for a turkey sandwich, she gave him an expectant look.

"So tell me what it is we need to talk about that couldn't be done over the phone. I have to be back in forty-five minutes."

Despite his tension, a grin tugged at his lips. "Nothing like the direct approach."

She lifted one shoulder. "I don't believe in beating around the bush."

"Yeah. I noticed." When a soft blush bloomed on her cheeks, he tried to mitigate any implied criticism. "And for the record, I prefer candor."

She acknowledged his caveat with a quick dip of her head and waited him out.

Stalling, Craig took a sip of water. There wasn't any way to spin this that would put him in a favorable light, and his ego balked at admitting his failings as a father. But his pride was expendable, he reminded himself. Vicki's welfare had to come first.

As he set the water glass carefully back in the ring it had left on the polished wooden table, he folded his hands in front of him. "I assume Edith told you the basics. I'm a single parent, raising a four-year-old daughter."

"Yes."

"In our world today, my situation isn't unique. But the reason for it is." He clenched his fingers, watching as the knuckles whitened. "My wife and son were killed in a boating accident when I was stationed in Hawaii. It happened three years ago. Vicki was fourteen months old."

Shock rippled across her face. "Oh, Craig…I'm so sorry."

"Thanks." He cleared his throat and took another sip of water. "Since then, Vicki has been cared for by nannies in the condo I rented in Washington. In the gap between nannies, my mother filled in."

He hesitated. Braced himself. Plunged in. "In my grief, I shut myself off from my daughter. She has many of my wife's features, and every time I looked at her she reminded me of everything I'd lost. So I delegated her care to other people. Now, we have almost no connection. But I want to change that. That's one of the reasons I came to Nantucket. For a fresh start."

He leaned forward intently. "I know it will be an uphill battle, Kate. But I want to give it my best shot. I don't intend to work the long hours I did in Washington, but I do need someone to watch her during the workday. I can go with the day care I have lined up if necessary, but I think she'd do much better with personal attention from someone like Edith. And the icing on the cake would be Maddie. Vicki's never had a playmate, and I think it would do her a world of good to have a friend her own age. So I'm hoping you'll consider my request. For my daughter's sake."

Several beats of silence ticked by as Kate studied him. At last she took a deep breath. "That's quite a story."

"I know." And she hadn't even heard half of it. But that could come later. Maybe.

The waiter delivered their food, giving them both a chance to regroup. Kate picked up her spoon. Dipped it in her soup. Set it down.

For a long moment she regarded him with those intelligent, insightful green eyes. "I'll tell you what. Let's give it a try. If the girls don't get along, or some other problems arise, we can revisit it. Does that work for you?"

Relief poured through him. "Yes. And thank you."

Her expression softened. "I know how tough it is to be a single parent."

"Edith told me you'd lost your husband." He didn't mention the information he'd received from Maddie. "You've done a better job of coping than I have. Maddie seems happy and well-adjusted."

A whisper of a smile touched her lips. "She knows she's loved. That makes all the difference."

His stomach knotted. "That's exactly where I've failed with Vicki."

"Grief can be very destructive."

So could guilt. But his spoken response was different.

"You're cutting me way too much slack. I was selfish and wrapped up in my own anguish. Vicki deserved better. But I'm determined to do whatever I can to make things right with her. If she'll give me the chance."

"Children are very forgiving creatures."

"I hope you're right. In fact, I'm counting on that." He gestured toward her bowl. "Now eat your soup before it gets cold or you run out of time."

She picked up her spoon again. "When is Vicki coming?"

"I'm flying to Wisconsin to pick her up this weekend."

"So you'll need Edith starting a week from today?"

"Yes. I'll give her a call to finalize the arrangements."

They ate in silence as Craig tried to think of some innocuous topic to introduce to fill the sudden quiet. But he came up blank. Small talk didn't seem to fit their charged relationship.

In the end, Kate rescued him by spooning the last of her

chowder into her mouth and reaching for her purse. "Sorry to have to run. But it looks bad when the teachers are late."

A speck of the soup's cream base clung to the corner of her lips, and without thinking he reached for her napkin and gently wiped it away. At her muted gasp, however, he jerked his hand back and tucked it in his lap, willing the surge of heat on his neck to stay below his collar.

"Sorry." He tried for a smile. "There was a little misplaced quahog."

She positioned her purse in front of her chest. "Thanks. The kids would have had a field day with that. Teacher with egg— or in this case, chowder—on her face." She rose. "I guess I'll see you around."

Shooting him a quick, uncertain smile, she hurried toward the exit.

He stood, too, waiting until she disappeared through the door to retake his seat.

When he did, however, his focus wasn't on his barely touched sandwich…but on the faint traces of lipstick that clung to the napkin he'd dropped into his lap.

Fingering the square of linen, he thought about Kate's comment that Maddie knew she was loved. And how that made all the difference.

That wasn't true only for children, Craig reflected. Love had once made all the difference in his life, too, thanks to Nicole. And he yearned to find that kind of love again. To fill the empty space in his heart.

But that wasn't to be, thanks to the part of the story he hadn't told Kate.

The part that proved he never deserved to love—or be loved—again.

His appetite disappearing, he wadded up the napkin, set it on the table and rose, leaving the rest of his lunch—and his futile dreams—behind.

* * *

Kate took a discreet peek at her watch as Larry Atkins tried to move through the faculty meeting agenda at a brisk pace. But they'd gotten bogged down over a discussion about the deadline for final grades, and now she was late picking up Maddie. Not that Edith would mind. But Maddie would. Her daughter usually watched for her at the window.

Of course, starting next week, she might be less anxious for her mother's return——assuming she got along with Craig's daughter. And there was no reason to think she wouldn't. Not if the daughter was half as charming as the father.

Hard to believe that ten days ago she'd thought of the lieutenant as stuffy and arrogant, Kate mused. After their lunch today, she viewed him as grieving and guilt-ridden.

She also empathized with his loss and understood his guilt. By his own admission, he hadn't handled his daughter well. Yet she admired him for his willingness to acknowledge his shortcomings—and for taking steps to make things right. That spoke well of his character, and—

"Kate? Is that a possibility?"

At Larry's prompt, she pulled herself back to the meeting. All eyes were aimed at her, and warmth spilled onto her cheeks. "Sorry. I missed the question."

"I was telling everyone that our speaker for the career assembly tomorrow bailed, and I asked if anyone knew of a good replacement. Clarie mentioned she'd seen you at lunch today with the new Coast Guard commander, and she thought you might be willing to ask him to fill in."

Thanks a lot, Clarie, Kate telegraphed to her coworker.

The other teacher smirked.

"I don't really know him very well, Larry. Our paths have crossed a few times, that's all."

The principal sighed and ran his fingers through his thinning hair. "We're in a bind here, Kate. I can do a cold call, but it would be less awkward for both parties if you could put out a feeler. I can follow up with details if he's willing to consider it."

"It's such short notice," Kate stalled, trying to think of a diplomatic way to refuse. Considering how his simple touch of her lips at lunch with her napkin had disrupted her pulse, it would be safer to limit contact with the lieutenant.

"But it can't hurt to ask. A lot of these guys have canned speeches available for requests like these. It's just one phone call, Kate. I'll bring goodies from Downyflake to the teachers' lounge tomorrow if you'll do this."

A chorus of voices erupted, encouraging her to grant the principal's request, and she finally capitulated.

"Okay, fine. I'll call him. But I'm not making any promises."

"Good enough. Any other business?" When no one spoke, Larry ended the meeting. "I'll wait to hear from you, Kate. You have my home number if you don't reach him until later."

As the group dispersed, Clarie ambled over. "Sorry to put you on the spot. But I didn't think it would be a big deal. Things looked pretty cozy between you and the lieutenant." She leaned closer and lowered her voice. "So what's the scoop on your rendezvous?"

Stuffing her calendar and notebook into her satchel, Kate twisted the latch and stood. "There is no scoop. He wanted to talk to me about having Edith watch his daughter, like she watches Maddie."

The other woman's face fell. "He's married?"

Kate was tempted to lie but resisted. Besides, she'd be found out eventually. "Was. His wife died."

"Yeah? What happened?"

"I didn't get a lot of detail." Kate headed toward the door.

"So you're not interested in him, right?" Clarie called after her.

"Right."

That was the truth, Kate tried to tell herself as she pushed through the door. The pursuit of a new relationship wasn't on her agenda.

But as the door closed behind her and she went to make the call, she couldn't help wondering what it would be like to be romanced by the tall, broad-shouldered lieutenant with the amazing blue eyes.

As she stood at the window of the teachers' lounge the next day, watching the relentless rain slash through the dreary landscape, Kate sighed and telegraphed a silent question to the gray heavens: *How come it's never easy, Lord?*

No answer came.

None was expected.

God didn't answer questions like that with writing on the sky or in thunderbolts. It all came down to a matter of trust, of believing that all things worked together for good. She knew that. Accepted it.

But she wasn't seeing a whole lot of good in the sudden demise of the timing belt on her twelve-year-old Civic—and the accompanying several-hundred-dollar expense.

Why couldn't it have waited another six weeks to die? she lamented, shoving her hands into the pockets of her gray slacks. Once the charter season kicked in, the cost wouldn't be such an issue. But her bank balance was often anemic by April. This year more than usual, thanks to an extra trip to the pediatric pulmonologist and some high-priced tests and medications for Maddie. Her health insurance covered a good percentage of those expenses—but not enough. She'd be operating on fumes after this.

Chester, bless his heart, had offered to do what he could when he'd dropped her off at school today. For once, though, she doubted his mechanical skills would be able to save her.

He was a great tinkerer, but he wasn't equipped to pull off such a major repair.

She'd find a way to deal with the expense, though. She always did. Because moving away from the island, as her parents had been forced to do when the cost of living skyrocketed, wasn't an option.

"Hey, Kate, aren't you going to the assembly? After all, you got our speaker."

At Clarie's question, Kate turned her back on the dreary scene outside as two other teachers joined her in the lounge.

"My sole contribution was a thirty-second call. Larry took it from there."

"Personally, I can't imagine any available woman *not* going." Steph, who taught history, responded to Clarie's question as she rested her hand on the bulge in her tummy. "If I wasn't already spoken for, and motherhood wasn't imminent, I'd sit front and center. Did you get a load of that guy?"

"Yeah." Clarie responded to Steph's question. "What a hunk!"

"I didn't know you ladies were talking about me." Hank Kraus, who taught social studies, pushed through the door with a grin, smoothing down his thinning salt-and-pepper hair and patting his slight paunch.

"Cute, Hank." Clarie smirked at him. "We were talking about today's speaker for the career opportunities assembly."

"Oh, yeah. I saw him in the lobby. Impressive uniform."

"You are staying, aren't you?" Clarie aimed her query at Kate as she rummaged in her purse for her lipstick.

"For a few minutes anyway. But I'll probably sit in the back and sneak out early. I have to deal with some car problems."

"I, for one, being available, interested and attractive, intend to sit in the first row," Clarie announced as she applied her lipstick.

"Two out of three isn't bad." Hank ducked as Clarie aimed a playful swat in his direction.

Ten minutes later, after a quick stop in the ladies' room to run a comb through her hair and touch up her own lipstick, Kate headed for the auditorium, choosing the seat closest to the door in the last row. As she settled in, the principal strode onto the stage.

"Quiet, please. We're ready to begin." He waited until the teenage chatter died down before launching into his introduction. "Ladies and gentlemen, today we were supposed to wrap up our career series with a navy pilot. I know a lot of you were looking forward to hearing from him. However, another commitment has kept him from joining us."

A collective groan rolled through the room, and the principal held up his hands. "However, our new Coast Guard commander graciously agreed to step in and take his place. Some of you may have heard about his previous position at headquarters. But you may not be aware of the exciting life he led before he took a desk job in Washington. Today he's going to share with us some of his experiences as a Coast Guard rescue swimmer. Please welcome Lieutenant Craig Cole."

As Craig rose from a seat in the first row, his dark blue dress uniform drawing attention to his broad, powerful shoulders, Kate wanted to sink through the floor. The man had been a rescue swimmer. A member of an elite group of well-trained men and women in superb condition who jumped out of helicopters into raging seas to save lives.

And she'd hammered him about swimming off Great Point.

Mortified, Kate considered sneaking out the back door. But before she could make her move, Craig stepped behind the microphone and turned, displaying an impressive array of ribbons above his left pocket.

And once he began speaking, he held every person in the auditorium—Kate included—spellbound with his stories of dramatic rescues in both the icy Arctic waters off Alaska, where he'd begun his career, and in the tropical seas off Hawaii, which held their own terrors for the unsuspecting.

During the forty-minute presentation, Kate learned that there were only three hundred rescue swimmers among the thirty-eight thousand men and women on active duty in the Coast Guard; that the attrition rate in the rigorous swimmer training school was higher than fifty percent; and that the term bingo might be a good thing in reference to a square piece of cardboard containing numbers and letters, but it was a very bad thing for a search and rescue team in a Jayhawk.

She learned something else, as well.

Craig Cole was a true hero.

Although he downplayed his role in the rescue operations he described, always giving credit to the entire Jayhawk team, Kate knew that when the flight mechanic gave the signal, he was the one who'd jumped into the churning sea. This was a man who'd put his life on the line to save others. Countless times. Craig might have come to Nantucket from a desk job in Washington, but he'd earned his stripes the hard way.

Impressed didn't come close to describing Kate's reaction.

Yet…there was a disconnect, she suddenly realized.

In many of the rescue scenarios he'd described, Craig had talked about the need for flexibility, quick thinking and improvisation. About the importance of modifying procedures to suit unique situations not covered by the cut-and-dried rulebook. But since his arrival in Nantucket, he'd been hard-nosed about enforcing minor safety regulations. Everything had to be done precisely by the book, no matter the circumstances. She hadn't been his only victim, as she'd later discovered.

It didn't make sense.

However, now wasn't the time to try and figure it out, she decided, as he wrapped up his talk. Not if she wanted to make a quick exit.

As the applause died down and a cluster of students surged

forward to talk to the commander, Kate used the opportunity to slip out the door.

Moving down the hall a short distance, she pulled out her cell phone and called Edith. Chester had told her to let him know whenever she was ready to leave, and although the heavy rain might slow him a little, he could make the trip in less than ten minutes. He'd arrive long before Craig finished answering questions from the interested students.

A busy signal beeped over the line. Waiting sixty seconds, she tried again. Still busy. It had to be Edith, Kate concluded. Chester didn't like telephones, preferring face-to-face conversations. As a result, his calls rarely lasted more than a minute.

Frowning, Kate tapped her foot. If Edith's conversation dragged on too long, she could always duck into the ladies' room.

At least she wouldn't have to worry about running into the lieutenant there.

From his position in the front of the auditorium, surrounded by a large group of students clamoring for his attention, Craig caught a quick glimpse of fiery red hair in the back of the room. Kate. Craning his neck, he looked again. But she'd vanished.

"Do you need to talk to Ms. MacDonald?"

The astute question from a gangly teen juggling a knapsack who'd zoned in on Craig's line of sight refocused his attention.

"No. She seemed to be in a hurry."

"Yeah. She's got a lot on her plate. But she's never too busy to talk to the students or walk us through a tough assignment. She's awesome."

Considering she was raising her daughter alone, ran a charter fishing operation —also alone—and taught school, the student had picked a good adjective to describe her, Craig concurred.

"Are there any women rescue swimmers, Lieutenant?"

The query from an athletic-looking girl forced him to switch gears. "Yes. A few."

For the next fifteen minutes he fielded questions, until the principal stepped forward and reminded the students their rides were waiting and that Craig had to get back to work.

"I'll tell you what. If any of you have other questions, give me a call at my office. I'll be happy to answer them." He withdrew some business cards from his pocket and passed them around.

As the students broke up, he shook hands with the principal, accepted the man's thanks for being a last-minute substitute and headed toward the door where Kate had disappeared. But he wasn't surprised when a quick scan of the hall revealed no one with red hair.

Stifling a surge of disappointment, he strode toward the entrance.

"Lieutenant!"

At the summons, he turned. A thirty-something blonde smiled and approached.

"I'm Clarie Peterson." She extended her hand. "I teach math here, and I wanted to say I thought your talk was very informative and inspiring."

"Thank you." He retrieved his hand with a gentle tug.

"Of course, I'm sure you barely scratched the surface in the short amount of time you had. I, for one, would be fascinated to hear more of your stories. I wondered if I might buy you a cup of coffee sometime?"

Keeping his PR smile in place, Craig searched for a diplomatic way to refuse the invitation. "I'm glad you enjoyed the presentation, Ms. Peterson. And that's a very kind offer. The thing is, I'm still learning the ropes at the station, and—"

The ladies' room door opened, and Craig suddenly found himself looking into a pair of startled green eyes below a flaming halo of hair. Sending a fervent thank-you heavenward, his smile changed from PR to the real thing.

"Kate. I was hoping to catch you. Do you have a minute?" He telegraphed a silent SOS, praying she'd catch the signal.

Her gaze flickered to Clarie, and she smiled back at him. "Sure."

Message received. *Thank you, Lord!*

The blonde's eyes narrowed as she sized them up.

"Clarie!" Hank waved from down the hall. "We need to run or we'll be late for the get-together at Brotherhood."

"I'll be there in a sec," Clarie called over her shoulder. Tipping her head, she gave Craig a forced smile. "The offer of coffee stands. You can always reach me through the school. See you later, Kate."

Not until she disappeared around the corner did Craig speak. "Thank you."

Kate gave him an empathetic smile. "Clarie can come on a little strong. She got divorced about three years ago and lately she's been on the prowl. But the pickings are somewhat limited. So when someone like you shows up…" She shook her head, and her smile grew rueful. "A rescue swimmer, no less. I'm embarrassed about my faux pas at Great Point."

"Don't be. You were right." He shoved one hand in the pocket of his slacks. "I took a foolish chance. And your dressing-down was a wake-up call. You'll be happy to know I've been more prudent in my swimming locations since then."

"Thanks for being gracious about it. Anyway, Clarie's a lovely person. You'd enjoy her company."

"I'm not in the market." Without giving Kate a chance to linger on that comment, he changed subjects. "The guy who called your friend mentioned a gathering. I hope I'm not keeping you from a social engagement."

"No. Making small talk isn't my thing. Besides, my time is

too—" The ring of her cell phone cut her off, and she retrieved it from her purse. "Would you excuse me for a second?"

"No problem."

As Craig listened to the one-sided conversation, it became clear Kate was relying on Chester to pick her up. Leaning over, he spoke close to her ear. "Do you need a ride?"

She shot him a quick glance. Hesitated. "Can you hold a minute, Edith?" Pressing the mute button, she shook her head. "Thanks. I've got it covered."

"But I'm here. Chester's not. Why not save him a trip on this rainy day? Besides—" he gave her what he hoped was a persuasive smile "—you rescued me a few minutes ago. One good turn deserves another."

Craig wasn't sure why he was pushing—other than the fact he liked being around Kate MacDonald. In her presence, he felt more alive than he had in three long years. She was engaging, energizing and appealing—not to mention lovely.

In other words, he was attracted to her.

And that was dangerous. He ought to be backing off, not forging ahead. That would be the smart thing to do.

The flicker of indecision in her eyes told him she was uncertain, too. If he gave her an excuse to decline, he suspected she'd take it.

But he didn't.

For several long moments she studied him. Then she spoke into the phone. "Tell Chester he can stay dry, Edith. I have a ride."

Leaving Craig to wonder if he'd just made a big mistake.

Chapter Six

Five minutes later, as Craig pulled up in front of the school and Kate dashed for his car, the word *mistake* kept repeating in her mind like a stuck needle on one of the old vinyl records her father used to play.

Spending time with the handsome lieutenant was not a good idea.

With each encounter, his appeal grew. And that was scary. It could undermine her resolve to steer clear of romance. When Mac had died, a big chunk of her heart had died, too. A person could only take so much loss, and she'd reached her limit.

At least the ride home was short, she reassured herself as Craig slowed to a stop and pushed open the passenger door.

Kate slid in. "Wow! What a day to forget my umbrella."

"Considering Nantucket's reputation as a resort destination, I have to admit I'm surprised by the weather."

"It's a summer resort. And around here, summer doesn't get a good grip until June or July. The rest of the year can be pretty much like this. Or worse." She clicked her seat belt into place as he accelerated. "Take a right. It's not very far." His medal-bedecked jacket was gone, she noted, replaced by a rugged, off-white fisherman sweater.

Catching her inspection, he grinned and answered her unspoken question. "I ditch the jacket as soon as possible after official functions. It's a high-maintenance garment. So, may I assume your need for a ride indicates car problems?"

"You may. My timing belt's shot."

He grimaced. "Ouch. That's an expensive repair."

"Tell me about it." Although she tried to keep her tone conversational, a note of discouragement crept into her voice. She hoped Craig wouldn't pick up on it.

But she wasn't surprised when he did. The man had razor-sharp instincts.

"I suppose managing a budget with two seasonal careers has its challenges."

"That's a polite way to put it. Take a left at the next corner."

"Have you ever considered teaching full-time?"

"Yes. I was offered a full-time position two years ago. But I'd lose two of my most lucrative fishing months. And it would pretty much even out income-wise. The group insurance would be nice because my premiums would be lower, but I like the flexibility of being available for Maddie." She sighed and shook her head. "There's just no easy answer."

He took a quick look at her, noting the determined set of her chin. He doubted there were many obstacles capable of stopping Kate from achieving any goal she set. Yet worry—and hard work—took a toll, as evidenced by her too-thin frame, the shadows beneath her lower lashes, the faint lines at the corners of her eyes. Spunk and resolve, much as he admired them, could exact a hefty price.

"Make a right. Then in two blocks make a left. I know the layout is a maze to newcomers, but it makes perfect sense to us natives."

"How long has your family lived here?"

"Almost two hundred years. We go back to the whaling days. My forefathers did very well on Nantucket, until kerosene and the Great Fire ended the glory days. Every generation since has had its struggles. Most of the family ended up moving to the mainland. It's tough for ordinary people to make a living on the island, especially in recent years."

He took a quick look at her, noting the shadow that crossed her face.

"Even my parents had to move," she continued, a touch of melancholy softening the words. "A few years ago they sold the house where I grew up and relocated to a small bungalow in North Carolina. But they didn't transplant well. Two years later, my mother suffered a fatal stroke. Eight months after that, my dad died of a heart attack."

Shocked, Craig digested this new information. In a handful of years, Kate had lost not only her husband, but both parents.

"It's the next street on the right. Lighthouse Lane."

Slowing, Craig turned into the tiny dead-end street containing a handful of houses. Most were a nice size, but in light of her comments about finances, he wasn't surprised when she directed him to a small clapboard cottage tucked between two of the grander homes.

She secured her purse on her shoulder. "Thanks for the lift. I know Chester appreciates it as much as I do."

"It was my pleasure." He shifted toward her as the rain continued to beat against the car, the rivulets of water acting like an opaque curtain, insulating them from the world. Only Kate's hair added color to the neutral palette around them. Even in the weak light, it sparked with life and vibrancy.

All at once, Craig was rocked by a powerful urge to touch those curls. To smooth away the shadows under her eyes. To twine his fingers with hers and assure her she didn't have to face her problems alone.

Where that urge came from, he had no idea. All he knew was that the force of it threatened to shatter the emotional control he'd mastered as a rescue swimmer—a control that had saved his life on numerous occasions. And that unnerved him. He relied on that control. *Needed* that control. It was what helped him survive—in the water and out. Nothing—and no one—had ever managed to shake it as quickly and thoroughly as Kate MacDonald. Worse, she'd done it without even trying.

As if sensing his inclination, Kate groped for the door handle. "Th-thanks again for the ride."

"Wait." His hand shot out, restraining her, and she turned to him with an almost panicked expression. Gentling his voice, he summoned up a stiff grin, trying to dispel the charged atmosphere. "I have an umbrella in the back. No sense getting drenched. Let me walk you to the door."

Without giving her a chance to refuse, he reached into the backseat for the umbrella, opened his door and stepped out into the driving rain.

He took as long as he dared circling the car, pretty certain that huddling with Kate under the umbrella wasn't going to help matters. Based on the trepidation in her face when he pulled her door open, she'd had the same thought. And her discreet but obvious effort to keep some distance between them while they walked down the flagstone path that led across the tiny front lawn was also telling.

As they approached the entrance, Craig tried to distract himself by focusing on the weathered clapboard cottage she called home, noting the sage-colored door and matching trim framing the windows that gave the house a rustic charm in keeping with the historic nature of the town. No porch or awning protected the front door from the weather, and he canted the umbrella over them as she dug in her satchel for her keys.

"I appreciate the ride." Her words came out in a breathless rush. "I'm already late picking up Maddie, and you saved me some time."

"Is she at Edith's house?"

"Yes." Kate motioned toward the two-story Federal-style clapboard home to the left. Painted yellow and adorned with black shutters, it boasted a small set of friendship stairs at right angles to the front door that allowed visitors to approach the landing from either side.

Although Edith's house was far grander than Kate's, it paled in comparison to the one on her right. Also two-story and constructed of clapboard, it was painted white. The black shutters, Greek Revival roofline with its deep frieze, and a small, white-pillared front porch gave it a stately air.

"That's The Devon Rose," Kate told him, noting the direction of his glance as she fitted the key into the lock. "The owner lives on the second floor and serves high tea every afternoon downstairs. Well…" She edged the door open.

"Would you like me to get Maddie for you? With this giant umbrella I might be able to keep her drier than you could. No sense having her catch a cold." A gust of wind spewed rain in their direction, and he adjusted the angle of the umbrella to compensate. "And if you have an extra blanket I could throw it over her as added protection."

After another brief hesitation, Kate nodded. "Okay. Come in while I get an afghan."

She pushed the door open, and Craig stepped inside behind her.

While the exterior of the cottage was in keeping with the Historic District Commission guidelines, great liberties had been taken with the interior, Craig realized. Instead of the warren of tiny chambers he'd expected, he found himself in a spacious, open room that brought the house into the twentieth century without compromising the character of the original dwelling.

Wide pine floorboards, complemented by exposed beams in the ceiling, ran the length of the large room to the right of the small entry space. In the front of the room, a comfortable-looking upholstered sofa and chairs were clustered around a fireplace. The wooden mantel had been painted a soft ochre, and an old-fashioned clock flanked by brass candlesticks stood in the center.

Further back, a dining space was defined by an area rug in a bold, contemporary pattern. A sturdy wooden table, bare except for a fruit-filled lightship basket in the center, was surrounded by four ladder-back chairs with woven rush seats. The walls were painted a soft white, adding to the feeling of airiness, and double French doors at the back of the room led outside.

"Very nice," Craig commented. "And not at all what I expected."

"Thanks. My husband and I inherited the cottage from his parents, but the original layout was pretty claustrophobic. We felt bad about tearing out century-old walls, but I like the result." Grabbing an afghan off the couch, Kate passed it to him. "I'll call Edith before you go so she can have Maddie ready."

While Kate retreated to the kitchen to place the call, Craig ambled around the living room, stopping to examine a striking painting of Nantucket moors that hung over the mantel. He turned as he heard her approach.

"This is extraordinary."

"I think so, too." She moved behind a wing chair and gripped the top. "My husband painted it."

Surprise arched one of Craig's eyebrows. "I didn't know he was an artist."

"That's what he did in the off season, while I taught. He was good enough to do it year-round, but he liked the variety of two occupations. And he said being out on the water doing the charters gave him ideas for paintings." A spasm of pain tightened her features. "I wish we'd kept more of his pieces."

"Did he sell at one of the local galleries?"

"Yes. As fast he could paint them. I only have two." Her

fingers tightened on the chair, rippling the smooth surface of the fabric. "We both thought he had plenty of years left to paint more."

Knowing he was stepping onto shaky ground, Craig asked the question anyway, his tone gentle. "What happened to him, Kate?"

She swallowed. Moistened her lips. "He had an undiagnosed congenital heart defect. Hypertrophic cardiomyopathy, if you want the official name. It's caused by an asymmetrical thickening of the walls of the heart, and it can trigger sudden cardiac arrest. You mostly hear about it in athletes. But Mac liked to go scalloping with friends in the off season, and that can be a pretty strenuous activity, too. He was…gone before they could get him back to shore."

At Kate's strained retelling of the tragedy that had changed her life, Craig's gut twisted. He knew what it felt like to be the recipient of that kind of devastating news. But Kate's story was even more heartbreaking than his, in some ways. As he'd learned from Maddie, she'd not only lost her husband, she'd lost the father of her unborn baby.

"I'm sorry." From experience, he knew the trite phrase did little to ease an aching heart. But he also knew there were no words that could provide solace.

"Thanks." She blinked and cleared her throat. "They say the good die young. That was the case with Mac. He was only forty-one. But you know, as much as I grieved over my own loss, I think I was sadder that Maddie would never know her father. She was born two weeks after he died."

The coil in Craig's gut tightened another notch. What must it have been like for Kate, so recently bereft of the man she'd loved, to give birth to the daughter they'd conceived? On what should have been an occasion of shared joy, she'd been alone, caught in a no-man's-land between grief and happiness as she mourned her husband and rejoiced in the birth of her daughter. At least he'd been with Nicole for the birth of both of their children. And he had good memories of their years as a family. Kate had neither.

"Anyway, I talked to Chester. Edith will meet you at the front door." She moved toward the fireplace and knelt. "I think I'll turn on the gas logs. It's an extravagance, but it always chases away the chill."

In her room, if not her heart, Craig speculated, watching as her fiery hair spilled over her shoulders and sparked to life in the light from the flickering flames.

It was clear she didn't expect Craig to respond to her revelation or to offer further condolence. And he was glad. There was nothing he could say to ease her pain. Only a warm embrace from a good friend, or someone she loved, would help. And he was neither.

But as he stepped through the door and popped open the umbrella to protect him from the storm, he couldn't help wishing he was.

By the time Craig returned—after an absence long enough to convince Kate that Edith had cornered him about the reason for the unexpected visit—she'd made some hot chocolate for Maddie.

From the small kitchen next to the eating area in the great room, she followed the sound of her daughter's giggles. Pausing in the doorway, she took in the scene.

Craig held Maddie in one arm, cuddling her against his sweater. The juxtaposition of his rugged attire and broad, powerful shoulders with her daughter's delicate frame tugged at a place deep in her heart. The scene made her think of the kind of homecomings she'd always envisioned with Mac.

The sudden pressure of tears behind her eyes took her off guard, and she retreated a step, listening to their conversation as she struggled to regain control of her emotions.

"I don't know," Craig told her daughter with mock seriousness. "I always heard little girls were made of sugar and spice. You better let your mommy check to see if you're melting from all that rain."

More giggles. "Little girls don't melt."

"Are you sure?"

"Yes. I've gotten wet before."

"Whew! That's a relief. I'd hate for you to dissolve into a gooey little puddle. What would I tell your mommy?"

Another eruption of giggles.

A smile tugged at Kate's lips, and blinking away the moisture that had obscured her vision, she stepped into the dining area. Craig was still holding Maddie. Her daughter's arms were around his neck, her cheek pressed against his sweater, and she didn't seem in any hurry to let go. Neither did Craig.

He caught sight of her and grinned. "Here we are."

"So I see. Maddie, honey, I made you some hot chocolate. It's in the kitchen."

"I like it here better." She snuggled closer to Craig's shoulder.

Kate folded her arms over her chest and smiled at Craig. "I think you've got a new friend."

"No complaints on my end. How about I carry you into the kitchen for that hot chocolate?" Craig directed the question to Maddie.

"Okay, I guess." She sniffled and wiped her nose on her sleeve. "Can you stay while I drink it?"

"Honey, I'm sure the lieutenant has to get back to work," Kate told her.

"To be honest, I'd planned to cut out after my talk today." He gave her an unrepentant grin. "One of the perks of being the boss."

Considering Edith was probably glued to the front window waiting to see how long Craig stayed, Kate wasn't thrilled by that news. The longer he hung around, the more difficult it would be to convince her matchmaking neighbor that his visit was nothing more than a simple ride home.

A sudden cough from Maddie, however, drove thoughts of Edith from Kate's mind. A minute ago she'd sniffled. Now she'd coughed. It could be nothing. But Kate had lived through too many asthma attacks to overlook even the most innocent-appearing symptoms. Nevertheless, she tried not to overreact. Being overprotective wasn't in Maddie's best interest, either.

Summoning up a smile, she led the way toward the table. "Okay. I'll bring it in here for you instead. Craig, would you like a soft drink?"

"I'm a hot chocolate man, myself." He winked at Maddie again, eliciting another giggle.

As she prepared Craig's drink, she heard her daughter cough again. *Please, Lord, no!* she prayed, her stomach tightening into an all-too-familiar knot. *Not tonight.*

Maddie was chattering away when Kate set the two mugs on the table. Craig was giving the youngster his full attention, and she was eating it up. But when another cough interrupted Maddie's effusive narration and her daughter wiped her nose again, Kate's concern escalated.

Pulling her chair closer to Maddie's, Kate took her seat and tried to think of anything that might have triggered an asthma attack. Nothing came to mind. She'd kept her out of the past week's cold air as much as possible, and when they had ventured out she'd been diligent about having Maddie wear her special ski mask. Edith wouldn't have exposed her to any of the known triggers, either. Yet the sudden coughing and runny nose were suspicious.

As Maddie told Craig all about the pictures she'd drawn at Edith's while her mother was teaching, Kate leaned closer, trying to determine if Maddie was having any trouble breathing. She thought she detected a slight wheezing. But perhaps it—

"Mommy, aren't you going to answer the lootenin's question?"

Her daughter's query registered on a peripheral level as Kate faced the hard truth. Maddie was definitely wheezing. And it was getting worse.

An asthma attack was on the way.

"I'm sorry…what did you ask?" Kate stood, trying to figure out how to get the nebulizer ready without alarming Maddie. Her daughter hated the machine—and what it represented. Even after three years of regular attacks, the episodes terrified her. Kate could relate. They terrified her, too. But she tried to hide her own apprehension and keep her daughter calm, knowing that panic, with its accompanying hyperventilation, would exacerbate an attack.

"Is everything okay?"

The quiet question from Craig told her he'd sensed her distress. She prayed Maddie hadn't.

"Maddie, honey, you finish your hot chocolate while the lieutenant helps me in the kitchen for a minute, okay?"

"Okay." She coughed and took another sip.

With a slight inclination of her head, Kate motioned to Craig. His eyes narrowed, and without a word he rose and followed her. Once out of Maddie's view, she turned to him. "I have a problem."

"I picked that up."

"Maddie has asthma, and I'm seeing warning signs of an approaching attack. I need to give her a nebulizer treatment and try to head it off."

She crossed the kitchen and opened the door of a lower cabinet, striving to remain calm, willing her hands to stop trembling. Wishing for once she could ask for help to get through this ordeal. Knowing she couldn't. It was just she and Maddie against the world. The way it had always been.

The way it would always be.

As she withdrew the nebulizer from the cabinet, she spoke over her shoulder. "This isn't a fun thing, Craig. You might want to head out before we get started. I'll explain to Maddie that you had to leave. It's okay."

And it was, Kate told herself. It had to be.

Even if her heart said otherwise.

Chapter Seven

As Craig watched Kate pull a piece of equipment out of the cabinet, he could tell she was trying to stay calm. The rigid lines of her body, however, along with her white-knuckled grip on the machine she was placing on the counter and the slight twitch at the corner of her mouth, betrayed her agitation. Yet he had no doubt she could handle this crisis alone, as she'd handled all the similar ones he assumed had come before.

But he didn't want her to have to manage this one by herself.

"I'd like to stay and help."

At his words, she went still for several long seconds. At first he thought she was going to refuse. Instead, when she turned, he caught the glimmer of tears in her eyes. "Thank you."

"Just tell me what to do."

She straightened her shoulders and went back to work. "The best way you can help is to try and keep Maddie calm. She knows these spur-of-the-moment treatments mean an attack is probably coming." She frowned as she washed her hands and began setting up the equipment. "I wish I knew what triggered this. I've been so careful about keeping her out of the cold and wind. And she knows better than to go near cats."

A cold knot formed in Craig's stomach and he froze. "What's the problem with cats?"

"She has a severe allergy to cat dander. And allergies are huge asthma triggers."

As the implications of Kate's explanation sank in, Craig felt as if someone had kicked him in the stomach.

For one brief instant he couldn't move. Then he went into action. Stripping off his sweater, he strode to the back door, opened it, and hurled the garment onto a sodden wooden bench a few feet away in the compact back yard.

When he turned back, Kate had stopped measuring medicine into the nebulizer cup and was staring at him as if he'd lost his mind.

A muscle clenched in his jaw, and he shoved his fingers through his hair. "I'm sorry, Kate. I'm the cause of Maddie's allergy attack."

Understanding dawned in her eyes. "You have a cat?"

"No. But I was at my executive petty officer's house last night for dinner, and they do. His kids kept wanting me to hold it, and I picked it up a few times to satisfy them. I was wearing that sweater." He jerked his thumb over his shoulder, toward the back yard.

Some of the color drained from her face, and she sped up her efforts to prepare the nebulizer, attaching the mask to a T-shaped elbow. "At least we're catching it early."

By her methodical, rote actions, Craig knew she'd been through this routine countless times. Yet he hated being the cause of a repeat performance. More than that, he hated the underlying shakiness in her voice.

"Let me grab the afghan. It was up against my sweater." Without waiting for a response, he retrieved it from the living room. "Where do you want this?"

"In the laundry basket. It's in that closet." She indicated a set of louvered doors at one end of the kitchen.

Craig deposited the blanket in the lidded container and rejoined her. "Do you want to do the treatment in here?"

"No. I usually sit on the couch and hold her. It helps keep her calm."

He moved to the sink and washed his hands, drying them on a paper towel. "Maybe I can distract her during the treatment. How long does it take?"

"About ten minutes."

"I finished my—" Maddie stopped in the doorway when she caught sight of the nebulizer. The rhythm of her breathing underwent an abrupt change, her deeper breaths giving way to shallow, quick puffs.

Moving beside her, Craig dropped down to her level as she began to cough. Panic gripped her features, and he touched her cheek.

"Hey, sugar and spice." He winked at her and managed a smile. "Your mommy thinks it might be good for you to have a treatment. How about I tell you a story while you're having it?"

Her attention was riveted on the machine, and she didn't respond to his question. Reaching out, he grasped her thin arms in a gentle grip. "Maddie?" He waited until she focused on him. "Would you like to hear a story during the treatment?"

She gave a jerky nod. "Can I sit…on your l-lap?"

"I think that would be okay." He checked with Kate over his shoulder, and she dipped her head.

"Mommy, where's my…blanket?"

"I'll get it, honey. Craig, could you take her into the living room?"

Sweeping Maddie into his arms, he strode toward the couch and settled her on his lap.

Kate wasn't far behind. Handing a small, faded pink blanket to Maddie, she adjusted the mask on her daughter's face and turned on the compressor. "Okay, honey, now sit up straight and take long, slow, deep breaths through your mouth. That's it. Good girl."

Once Kate was satisfied with Maddie's inhalation, Craig launched into a tale about a rescue he'd participated in while stationed in Hawaii. It was one of his tamer stories, about saving a friendly Labrador, and he embellished it with as many colorful details as possible. Maddie clutched the blanket in one hand and clung to the sleeve of his dress shirt with the other, bunching the fabric in her fingers as she gave him her rapt attention. Kate knelt beside her, stroking her arm and murmuring encouragement.

When the cup containing the medicine was empty, Kate shut off the machine and removed the mask from Maddie's face. "That wasn't so bad, was it?" She took her daughter's hand and gently brushed back her hair.

"No." Maddie hiccupped and angled toward Craig, snuggling closer against his broad chest.

"How about you take a little rest before dinner?"

"But we have company."

"Not for long," Craig told her. "I'm going home in a few minutes."

"Will you come in first, while Mommy tucks me in?"

"If it's okay with your mommy."

"That's fine. Come on, honey." Taking her daughter's hand, Kate led her down the hall that opened off the great room.

He trailed behind, past a bathroom on the right and a darkened room on the left as they headed toward the last door at the end of the hall. A Disney princess lamp on the bedside table bathed the small room in a warm glow, and as Craig stepped inside he had a quick impression of pink walls, a woodland-fairy border and white wicker furniture.

As he juxtaposed this room against the one he'd prepared for Vicki, his stomach dropped to his toes. His daughter's had no personality. No warmth. No...joy.

It was a disaster.

"Craig? Is everything okay?"

Concern rippled through Kate's voice, penetrating his panic. "I was just thinking about the room I prepared for Vicki. It's…not good."

"Who's Vicki?"

"Vicki is the lieutenant's little girl," Kate explained to Maddie, aiming her next comment at Craig. "I hadn't told her yet."

"You have a little girl?" Maddie asked, wide-eyed.

"Sorry." Craig directed his apology to Kate.

She waved it aside. "It's okay." Refocusing on Maddie, she smiled. "It was going to be a surprise, honey. Vicki is the same age as you are. And Mrs. Shaw is going to watch her every day, too. So you'll have a friend."

Maddie's eyes lit up. "I always wanted a friend! When is she coming?"

"On Monday."

"How come her room isn't good?" Maddie addressed the question to Craig.

"I'm afraid I didn't know what little girls like. So it's pretty plain."

"We know what little girls like. We can help you make it better. Can't we, Mommy?"

Craig hadn't planned to initiate another encounter with Kate. It was too dangerous, in light of the electricity zipping between them. But considering the sad state of Vicki's room, he figured he'd better take any help he could get—from any source. No matter the risk.

"I know you're busy, but to be honest, I could use some advice. I want Vicki to feel welcome and wanted. And first impressions mean a lot."

Kate's eyes softened in compassion. "I think we could squeeze in a quick shopping trip. How about tomorrow night? We could meet you at your house and take a look at the room, then go from there."

Gratitude warmed his heart. "That would be great."

"We'll make it real pretty," Maddie promised, settling back on the pillows. "I'll think of all kinds of good things for you to buy."

Chuckling, Kate tucked her in. "Of that I have no doubt."

"Mommy, where's Raggedy Ann?"

"I left her in my bedroom, honey. Remember, I was patching her arm? I'll get her for you."

As Kate left the room, Maddie whispered to Craig. "You have to get lots of stuffed animals and dolls. And fairy-tale books. And sparkly barrettes. And a pretty bedspread with princesses and—"

"Maddie." Kate reentered the room and tucked the doll next to the little girl. "We'll talk about all this later, while we eat dinner. You need to rest for a little while." She rolled her eyes at Craig. "Like that's going to happen."

"See you tomorrow, Lootenin."

"Good night, Maddie. You keep thinking of everything we should put on our list."

"I will. Don't worry."

With a grin, Craig stepped into the hall. As Kate lingered to turn off the bedside light and answer one more question from her daughter, he strolled down the narrow corridor toward the living room. She'd left the light on in her bedroom, he noted, slowing to scan it as he passed. It was a simple but cozy room, dominated by a brass bed covered with an intricately patterned quilt in shades of green. An antique dry sink with an oval mirror stood against one wall, and a carved wooden rocking chair with a seat cushion occupied the far corner.

But it was the painting between a pair of windows that caught—and held—his attention.

Kate stared back at him from the canvas, her lips tipped up in a Mona Lisa smile, her glorious red hair dancing in the wind as she stood on the deck of the *Lucy Sue*. Her hands were propped on her waist, the worn denim of her jeans outlining her shapely legs. She wore a cream-colored shirt, the cuffs of the long, full sleeves tight at her wrists. Backed by the white-capped cerulean sea and a cloudless blue sky, dominating the scene with a powerful presence, she again made him think of the Irish chieftain pirate Grace O'Malley.

There was no question in Craig's mind that this was the second Mac MacDonald painting Kate had kept.

Mesmerized, he admired her ready-to-take-on-the-world stance. Was captivated by the fire and passion glinting in her eyes—and the hint of humor and tenderness in their depths. Felt the energy and vitality radiating from her proud, confident bearing. The painting captured every nuance of her personality. Her grit, determination and strength. Her vibrancy and enthusiasm. Her deeply emotional, sometimes volatile, temperament.

This rendering depicted Kate in love. With the sea, with life—and with her husband.

Craig didn't know much about Mac MacDonald, other than his masterful ability to wield a paintbrush. But he did know they shared one attribute: an appreciation for the special woman who had joined him in the hallway.

Sidling around him, Kate reached in and flipped off the light.

"That's quite a painting." He wasn't about to pretend he hadn't noticed it.

"It was Mac's only portrait." She moved down the hall, her back to him.

"That's a shame. He had remarkable talent."

She threw a brief, melancholy smile at him over her shoulder. "He claimed he only had one portrait in him."

That might be true, Craig conceded, surveying the panoramic scene over the fireplace as he followed Kate into the living room. Capturing people's personality required a different talent than rendering a landscape. To do it well, you had to have a rapport with your subjects, know what made them tick, have intimate insights into their personalities. And you had to be able to translate all those things to canvas.

Kate's husband had accomplished that feat with her painting. But perhaps he would have been less successful with others. Perhaps love was the reason he'd done such a stellar job with Kate's portrait. Every brushstroke, every nuance of color, every decision of angle and perspective reflected his esteem and love for the woman who stood a few feet away.

"He may have been right," Craig acknowledged. "It's an amazing painting."

"It means a lot to me." She blinked and shoved her hands into her pockets, continuing in a tone that was a little too bright. "Thanks for helping with the treatment."

"Will she be okay?"

"For now. But the attack could escalate later. We may be in for a long night."

"Has she always had asthma?"

"Yes, though it took a while for the doctors to settle on the diagnosis."

"And there's no cure?"

"No. We just do the best we can to control it with medication. I'm hoping she outgrows it. My mom had it as a child, and she was fine when she got older. Maddie's pulmonologist in Boston is optimistic she'll follow the same pattern."

Craig absorbed this latest piece of news. Kate traveled to Boston because of Maddie's health issues. To see a pricey specialist, who no doubt ordered lots of expensive tests and prescribed costly medications.

"No wonder you struggle to make ends meet." He also now understood why she preferred a more flexible schedule rather than a full-time teaching position. It gave her the ability to be there for Maddie when the need arose. Even if it provided less in the way of financial security.

She looked toward the fire, giving him a view of her pensive profile and the slender column of her neck. "You have to play the hand you're dealt. It's all about choices."

"Not everyone makes good ones." He raked his fingers through his hair and shook his head. "And Vicki suffered because I didn't. I have a lot to make up for with her. And I don't even know how to start."

She turned back to him, the firelight warming her skin, her voice soft. "Yes, you do. I've watched you with Maddie. You have a natural instinct with children. Maddie's shy with most people, but she connected with you right away. Vicki will do the same, if you give her a chance. Just follow your heart and love her. That's all it takes, Craig. Love is a powerful healer. It can work miracles."

Could it heal him, too? he wondered, taking in every nuance of Kate's lovely, earnest face. Could the love of a woman like Kate fill the dark, empty places in his heart and his soul?

"Do you really believe that?" His question came out gentle. Personal.

She retreated a step and gripped the back of the chair beside her. "Are we still talking about Vicki?"

Her direct question deserved a direct answer. "No."

She folded her arms across her chest. "Love among adults is more…complicated. And not always wise. But yes…in the right circumstances, I believe in its power to transform lives." She swallowed and hugged herself tighter. "Just in case you're…interested, Craig, you need to know that I'm not in the market for romance."

"Why not?"

"I loved Mac with every fiber of my being. He became part of me. When he died, that part of me died, too. I couldn't risk going through that again."

"I didn't think fear was part of your vocabulary. You strike me as a very strong woman."

The hint of a rueful smile tugged at her lips. "Strength and fear aren't mutually exclusive." Then she turned the tables on him. "What about you? Do you believe in the power of love?"

"For others, yes. For me, no."

She tipped her head. "Why not?"

He studied her in silence, debating how much to reveal. He'd never shared the full story of his tragic loss with anyone. He'd been too ashamed. But this woman, who'd known more than her share of loss and pain, might understand.

Besides, given the electricity between them, she needed to know that even if she changed her mind about romance, he wasn't the man for her.

"Would you like to sit for a minute?" He gestured toward the couch in front of the fireplace.

Without a word, she moved toward it, perching on one arm. He took the opposite side, clasped his hands between his knees and leaned forward, focusing on the flickering flames. "You already know that my wife and son were killed in a boating accident in Hawaii three years ago. What you don't know is…" He sucked in a deep breath. "It was my fault."

In the silence that followed, he didn't have to look up to know that shock had wiped the expression from her face.

When at last she spoke, her words were laced with confusion. "I don't understand."

"If I'd been more diligent, my wife and son would be alive today." His voice rasped as he dragged the pain-etched words from the dark crevice in his soul where they'd been buried for three long years.

"But…that doesn't make sense. I haven't known you long, but I can't reconcile your conclusion with the responsible, conscientious behavior I've seen since we met. I can't believe what you're saying is true."

"Believe it."

"But…you're not the negligent type, Craig. If anything, you're too thorough."

"Not that day. And all it takes is one slip to saddle you with a lifetime of regret."

"What happened?" She leaned forward. He could see her in his peripheral vision, but he couldn't make eye contact. Not until he got through this.

"My wife was the daughter of a career navy man, and she knew her way around boats and the ocean. Her attention to safety was one of the reasons I never worried when she took Aaron out on our small sailboat. She was usually more careful than I was."

"The day it happened I was on duty in the search and rescue command center. I'd given up rescue swimming six years earlier, when Aaron was born, figuring it was too dangerous for a family man." A mirthless smile twisted his lips. "Ironic, isn't it? I gave up my risky job to protect myself from the sea, yet they were the ones the sea claimed.

"Anyway, we'd had a report of some minor seismic activity in the Aleutian Trench that morning. Not significant enough to generate a tsunami warning, although we were watching it. I considered alerting Nicole, but she hadn't said anything about taking the boat out and I got busy. Mistake number one."

He massaged his brow, then reclasped his hands. "To make matters worse, I'd taken the adult-size life jackets out of our sailboat the night before. I'd intended to replace them the next day with new ones I was going to pick up on my way home from work. Again, I neglected to tell that to Nicole. Mistake number two.

"Early that afternoon, we began getting calls about a moderate-size rogue wave offshore. Shortly after that, a report came in of a capsized pleasure boat. Our boat." He swallowed, blinking several times to clear the moisture from his eyes. "By the time a rescue team arrived, it was too late.

Aaron had his life jacket on, but he'd been trapped inside the cabin when the boat turtled. Nicole had suffered a blow to the head, probably from the boom. She didn't have a life jacket, thanks to me. They both drowned."

Only the steady ticking of the clock on the mantel broke the sudden, oppressive silence in the room.

"Oh, Craig." Kate's voice was laced with tears when at last she spoke. "I can't begin to imagine what you went through."

He dropped his head and focused on the complex grain pattern in the flooring beneath his feet. "Words can't describe the anguish. And now you know why I don't deserve a second chance."

"But…the mistakes weren't all yours. If your son was wearing his life jacket, your wife must have known the adult jackets were missing. Besides, very few flotation devices will prevent an unconscious person from drowning."

"If Nicole was only dazed, it might have saved her. And if I'd told her about the seismic activity, she would never have gone out in the first place."

Silence filled the room before she spoke in a quiet voice. "Now I understand the motivation behind your overzealous safety program here. But Craig, you can't plan for every contingency. Life doesn't work that way. The accident was the result of a tragic sequence of events. No one would blame you."

He turned toward her at last. To his relief, there was compassion in her eyes. But that didn't change the facts. Or dilute his culpability. "*I* blame me. And I'll carry that burden of guilt for the rest of my life."

"You could give it to God instead."

He shook his head at her gentle suggestion. "I know that's supposed to work in theory. But I've tried. It won't go away."

"Maybe the real problem is that you can't forgive yourself."

"Maybe." He drew a steadying breath. "But I don't see that changing."

He watched her, wishing he could find a way to let the guilt go. To open himself to the kind of love a woman like Kate could offer. To seek comfort and healing in her loving arms.

Yet neither of them was looking for romance.

Suddenly exhausted, he rose. "I need to leave."

"Thanks for your help with the asthma attack."

"I caused it."

"Not on purpose." She rose, too. "Just like you didn't cause the boating accident on purpose."

"The consequences of that were tragic, though." He moved toward the door to retrieve his umbrella.

She stayed by the couch, bracing her hands behind her as she leaned on the back. And Craig found himself wishing he had Mac's talent. He'd love to capture her as she was now, backlit by the dancing flames in the fireplace, her eyes soft with compassion. It was a different view of Kate than the one Mac had painted. But it was equally powerful and true.

"Is the offer of help with Vicki's room still on the table?"

"Of course. How about if we show up around six o'clock?"

"That works for me." He twisted the doorknob. "I hope you have a quiet night."

"Thanks. So do I."

The rain continued to beat a staccato rhythm on the pavement as he stepped outside, and Craig dipped his head as he jogged toward the car.

Sliding into the driver's seat, he paused to savor the golden light spilling from the windows of Kate's house. Tonight, in her small cottage, he'd felt more at home than he had anywhere in the past three years. His rented condo in Washington had been sterile and impersonal. The house he now occupied felt cavernous. To him, it was just a place to sleep. Not a home.

But he needed to make it one, he reminded himself. For Vicki's sake. And he needed to create a family, even if it was never more than the two of them.

Two weeks ago that had seemed like an overwhelming task. Far more intimidating than any of the dangerous, roiling seas he'd dropped into during his days as a rescue swimmer.

Yet thanks to a feisty charter captain and her charming daughter, he no longer felt adrift. Kate and Maddie were living proof that two people could be a family. And with their assistance—and their example to follow—he was hopeful he could give Vicki the kind of loving home she deserved.

As he put the car in gear and headed toward the house he would soon occupy with his daughter, he forced himself to put aside his own loneliness and focus on the blessings he'd received since coming to Nantucket. He liked his work. He'd found a welcoming faith community and taken the first steps to reconnecting with the Lord. And in Kate and Maddie and Edith and Chester, he'd begun to build a support system. Things were looking up.

Nevertheless, he still said a silent prayer for God's grace to continue to fill his days and for courage to carry on. For life—like the sea—was rarely placid for long. And he wanted to be prepared for any turbulent waters that lay ahead.

Chapter Eight

"It's pretty pathetic, isn't it?"

At Craig's question, Kate scanned Vicki's bedroom. A matching white headboard, small dresser and nightstand were set atop a bland beige carpet. Utilitarian mini blinds hung at the two windows. A navy blue blanket covered the twin bed, which had been made with military precision. The walls were white and bare, the top of the dresser empty. A brass lamp stood on the nightstand. The only youthful touch was a lonesome teddy bear that rested against the white case of the pillow on the bed.

As she tried to come up with a diplomatic comment on the Spartan furnishings, her daughter stepped in with a single-word assessment.

"Yuck."

"Maddie!" Kate felt her cheeks grow warm. "That's not polite."

"But it's true." Craig sent the little girl a reassuring smile as he shoved his hands into his pockets. "Thank you for being honest, Maddie. So where do we start?"

Kate pulled a measuring tape out of her purse, trying to ignore the muscular forearms revealed below the rolled-up sleeves of his cotton shirt. "I need to measure the windows."

"I can do that. Without a ladder, too." He winked at her and took the measuring tape, the brush of his fingers against hers sending a tingle all the way to her toes.

Backing up a step, Kate dipped her head to hide the telltale flush that had once again warmed her cheeks, digging in her purse for a notebook. "If you read off the measurements, I'll jot them down."

Once that was accomplished, she tucked the notebook back in her purse. "I think we can do this in two or three stops. How do you feel about painting?"

"On a scale of one to ten, I'd give it a two. But I don't mind wielding a brush for a couple of hours if you think that will help. What color did you have in mind?"

"Pink," Maddie chimed in. "That's the bestest color."

Craig grinned. "Pink it is, then. Shall we, ladies?"

As they exited the room, Maddie tugged on Kate's hand. "I have to go potty, Mommy."

"First door on the right," Craig told Kate. "I'll wait for you in the kitchen."

Maddie kept up a running commentary as she used the bathroom and washed her hands. When she finished, Kate opened the door, only to have Maddie head in the wrong direction.

"This way, sweetie." She went to retrieve her, smiling as she tucked the little girl's hand in hers. "It's easy to get confused in a new place."

"It's kind of a big house, isn't it?"

"Yes." Compared to their snug cottage, anyway, Kate amended.

"Is that the lootenin's room?" Maddie stopped outside a room illuminated by a soft light.

Peeking in, Kate noted the queen-size bed, also neatly made. This room, too, was unadorned except for a photo on top of the dresser that faced the door. The light wasn't very bright, but Kate could tell it was a happy family group. A younger-looking Craig had his arm around a blond-haired woman, while a little boy with brown hair grinned back at the camera from between them.

Feeling as if she was spying, Kate hustled Maddie down the hall. "I guess it is, honey. Now we better hurry or bedtime will come before we have a chance to visit all the stores."

Craig was waiting for them in the kitchen, as promised. He'd donned a dark brown leather flight jacket that showed off his trim waist, and he reached for Maddie's coat as they approached.

While he helped her daughter slip her arms in and button up, Kate shrugged into her own quilted jacket and surveyed the kitchen. An empty can of soup stood on the counter by the sink, and a package of bagels rested next to a toaster. No other food was visible.

"If you're wondering, I did stock up on kid-friendly fare."

The man had an amazing ability to read minds, Kate concluded. "Kids can be pretty picky."

"I figured that." He secured the last button on Maddie's coat and stood. "I got peanut butter and jelly, white bread, cereal, hot dogs, pizza and ready-to-nuke chicken strips."

"Wow!" Maddie grinned up at him. "You did real good on the food part, Lootenin."

"Kid pleasers, for sure," Kate agreed. "You might want to throw in some fresh fruit, too."

"Pineapple," Maddie supplied. "And strawberries."

"Duly noted," Craig promised. "Shall we?"

For the next two hours, Kate hustled them from store to store, selecting a self-stick woodland-fairy border with matching curtains and comforter; pink sheets; a lamp with a whimsical winged fairy seated on a toadstool; a small combination toy chest and bookshelf, including books and toys to go with it; two colorful posters and, at Maddie's suggestion, a stuffed pink unicorn with a sparkly mane. On the practical front, Kate also helped Craig pick out a car seat. They'd transferred Maddie's to his car for the evening excursion.

Once back at Craig's house, she kept an eye on Maddie, who'd fallen asleep, as they carried in his purchases. After that chore was completed, Craig moved Maddie, car seat and all, back to Kate's car and strapped her in. Shutting the back door, he joined her on the driver's side.

"Will you be okay driving home?"

Fog had moved in during their ride back to his house, and it swirled around them now like a gossamer gray veil, obscuring his features. But she couldn't miss the concern in his tone. Nor stop the sudden rush of wistfulness that surged through her at his nearness.

"I've been all over this island in much worse conditions. And I don't have far to go." She tossed her purse onto the passenger-side seat, wishing she could think of some excuse to extend the evening. But it was late, Maddie was tired and she had a full teaching day tomorrow. It was time to say goodnight. "We better head out."

"Right." A couple of beats of silence passed. He didn't move. "Listen...I really appreciate your help tonight. The stuff you found— Vicki will love the room."

A smile tugged at her lips. "I had a lot of fun picking it out."

He gave a soft chuckle. "Spending other people's money can be quite a kick."

"I didn't mean it that way." Immediately regretting her impulsive statement, she shifted away and started to slide into the car. But his hand on her arm stopped her.

When she risked a peek at him, all traces of levity had vanished from his face and his eyes had darkened.

"I feel the same way, Kate. It's been years since family-type activities were part of my life. Tonight brought back happy memories."

"For me, too."

Somewhere in the distance, a boat whistle echoed in the fog. A long, plaintive sound that made Kate think of lost souls seeking safe harbor. Searching for peace and rest and safety.

Just as she—and the man standing inches away from her—were.

Both of them had sustained gut-wrenching losses. Both had struggled to deal with the aftermath of tragedy. But Craig was taking steps to get his life back on track. Like her, though, he'd reconciled himself to a solitary life.

Except she was beginning to waver, thanks to the man standing inches away from her.

As the fog intensified, cutting them off from the real world, Craig shifted closer.

Now, no more than a whisper separated them.

The night might be chilly. The undulating gray mist might be damp. But between them, the air was warm. Inviting.

Kate heard the soft chafe of his leather jacket as he lifted his arm. Felt the touch of his hand on her cheek. Let her eyes drift closed as an acute awareness rocked her.

He was going to kiss her.

And she wanted him to. Desperately.

Stunned by the power of her emotional response, Kate panicked. Slipping from his grasp, she ducked into the car and tried to fit the key in the lock. Her fingers were trembling so badly it took three tries. "I need to go."

"Kate…I'm sorry." Craig leaned down, and she forced herself to look at him. He seemed to have paled, though it might have been a trick of the swirling mist. But she wasn't imagining the distress that tightened his features.

"It's okay. And I really do have to go. There are a few things I need to take care of before I call it a night."

He didn't move. "Why do I feel as if I've just shot myself in the foot?"

Drawing a deep breath, Kate did her best to sound calm and in control. Even if she felt the opposite. "Honestly, Craig, it's fine. Tonight we were reminded of happier times, and emotions took over. It happens. It's no big deal." She turned the key in the ignition. "Have a safe trip to Wisconsin."

"Thanks." Several seconds of silence ticked by. Then he shut her door and backed away.

As Kate eased out of his driveway and pulled onto the street, she took one more look at him. He was standing where she'd left him, half obscured by the mist. In seconds he completely disappeared.

But the aftereffects of their near-kiss didn't disappear quite so easily. Despite what she'd told him, it *had* been a big deal. She hadn't kissed a man since Mac died. Hadn't even *considered* kissing a man. Any man, let alone one she'd met less than two weeks ago.

What in the world was going on?

The explanation she'd given Craig might account for tonight's incident. Anyone could get carried away. But it didn't account for her heightened emotions in general. At the most unemotional moments, an image of Craig, with his cobalt blue eyes and broad shoulders, would flash through her mind, distracting her from whatever she was trying to do—grade papers, fix dinner, balance her checkbook. For whatever reason, despite their rocky start, the man had gotten under her skin.

And as she drove through the enveloping mist that was erasing all the comforting landmarks of her familiar world, she had no idea how she was going to deal with it.

When a knock sounded on her back door Friday night as Kate unloaded the dishwasher, she wiped her hands on a towel and headed across the kitchen.

"Is Mrs. Shaw bringing us a treat?" Maddie looked up from her coloring book, her expression hopeful.

"How do you know it's Mrs. Shaw?"

"Because only the Shaws come to our back door. And Mr. Shaw's favorite TV program is on tonight."

Her four-year-old's deductive reasoning never failed to impress Kate. "Maybe."

But she hoped not. If her neighbor *was* bearing food, it meant she was either hunting for information or had news to impart. And lately, a certain lieutenant had been high on her list of newsworthy topics.

As Kate pulled the door open, the plate of oatmeal cookies in Edith's hand confirmed the purpose of her visit. But Kate was more distracted by the mass of damp wool dangling from the woman's other hand.

Craig's sweater.

She'd forgotten about him hurling it into the backyard the night of Maddie's asthma attack.

"I found this on your bench." Edith inclined her head toward the sweater and raised an eyebrow.

"That's the lootenin's," Maddie informed her, peeking under Kate's arm.

"It's a long story," Kate told Edith.

"I have plenty of time. What do you want me to do with this?" She hefted the sweater.

"Leave it on the porch. I'll deal with it later."

Dropping the garment, Edith handed Kate the plate of cookies and stepped inside. "These just came out of the oven."

"They look great. Go ahead and hang your coat on a peg. And wash your hands," Kate called over her shoulder as she carried the plate into the dining area.

"I washed them before I left the house."

"That sweater you picked up had a close encounter with a *c-a-t*."

"Ah." Edith moved to the sink and turned on the water. "That explains it."

She was drying her hands as Kate came back in. After pouring two mugs of coffee, Kate handed her one and filled a glass with milk for Maddie, who'd already homed in on the plate of cookies.

"These smell good, Mrs. Shaw," Maddie called from the dining area.

"Let's sample them, by all means." The older woman headed for the table and took her seat. Selecting a cookie, she broke off a piece and popped it in her mouth as she addressed Kate. "You told me about the episode Tuesday night, but not the cause."

She should have expected that lapse to come back and haunt her, Kate thought in chagrin as she perused the plate of cookies and selected one. Very little got by Edith.

"Are you talking about my asthma attack?" Maddie took another cookie.

Or her daughter.

"Yes, honey. To answer your question, Edith, I didn't see any reason to embarrass him. He felt bad enough as it was when he found out about the feline issue."

"The lootenin stayed for my treatment," Maddie volunteered. "He told me a story. It was fun while he was here."

"I'll bet." Edith stirred some cream into her coffee, flashing Kate a satisfied smile. "What a nice picture of domesticity."

"And Mommy and me went to his house to see Vicki's bedroom. It was yucky." Maddie wrinkled her nose and made a face. "But we went to the store with him and bought all kinds of good stuff to make it better."

Though Kate made a project out of stirring cream into her coffee, she could sense Edith's scrutiny.

"Maybe we can go see it after it's done," Maddie continued. "Can we, Mommy?"

"I don't think we'll have any reason to go back, Maddie. And you'll see Vicki every day at Mrs. Shaw's."

"But not the lootenin." Her face fell.

"Well now, I can think of another chance for you to see him. And to meet Vicki. That's why I came over. I called him earlier today and invited them for dinner Sunday night when they get back from Wisconsin. I'm hoping you both will come, too. I thought it might be nice for the girls to get to know each other with their parents present rather than just being thrown together on Monday morning."

Excitement brightened Maddie's eyes. "Can we, Mommy?"

After their unsettling parting on Tuesday, Kate wasn't in any hurry to be around the lieutenant again. But her neighbor's rationale was sound. A casual dinner in Edith's home would familiarize Vicki with both the setting and her caregiver. And it would give the girls a chance to get comfortable with each other, too.

She couldn't think of any logical reason to refuse.

And she didn't intend to share the illogical ones with Edith.

She was stuck. And judging by Edith's smug demeanor, the Lighthouse Lane matchmaker knew it.

"That sounds good, Edith. Count us in. Can I bring anything?"

Edith shook her head and rose. "Just your appetite. That's what I told Craig, too."

Kate shot her a suspicious look, but her neighbor's face was the picture of innocence as she leaned over to kiss Maddie's forehead. If there was a deeper meaning in her comment, she wasn't letting on.

"I'll see you both at church. Would you like to ride with us this week, Kate?"

"Sure. Thanks."

"Can we go to Downyflake afterward?" Maddie asked. "We could celebrate my new friend."

"Celebrating new friends." Edith mulled that over, her eyes twinkling. "I like that. Good idea, Maddie. After all, a person can never have too many friends." She aimed the last remark at Kate. "I'll let myself out."

As Kate watched the older woman disappear into the kitchen, there was no mistaking the meaning behind *that* comment.

Edith wasn't about to be abandon her matchmaking mission any time in the near future.

Less than three hours into his reunion with his daughter, Craig was having serious qualms about his ability to win her over.

As Lillian Cole refilled his coffee cup on Saturday night, he could feel Vicki scrutinizing him from the other side of the table—just as she'd been doing since his arrival. Usually with a solemn expression while gripping his mother's skirt. Not that he blamed her for her clinginess. Her grandmother had been the most constant loving presence in her young life. But her dubious appraisal unnerved him. It was clear his daughter didn't feel any more confident about his fatherhood abilities than he did.

"How about some pie?"

At Lillian's question, he forced himself to shift gears, somehow managing to summon up a smile. "Are you kidding? I've been salivating ever since I saw it on the counter." In truth, his appetite had vanished. But his mother had gone to a lot of effort to make a nice dinner, and he didn't want to disappoint her. "After all that fried chicken, though, I should resist. Pretty soon I'll need Roto-Rooter to clean out my arteries."

She gave him a playful nudge as she picked up his plate. "You don't need to worry. I've been eating fried chicken and apple pie for most of my seventy years and my cholesterol is perfect. I gave you good genes." She picked up Vicki's almost-untouched plate. "Are you finished, honey?"

The little girl nodded and tightened her grip on the ragged yellow blanket she'd been carrying around with her since his arrival. It reminded him of the one Maddie had.

"How about some pie?"

"Can I just have ice cream?"

"Sure enough. One extra-large scoop of vanilla coming up. Maybe with a little chocolate sauce?" Lillian smiled and winked at the child.

"Okay."

No answering smile, Craig noted. Just that big-eyed, forlorn stare in his direction.

The knot in his stomach tightened another notch.

While his mother did her best to keep a lighthearted conversation flowing during dessert, Vicki answered in monosyllables. And when it came time to get ready for bed, she wanted nothing to do with him, despite her grandmother's urging to let him handle the chore.

Craig had faced rejection before in his life. And he'd learned how to deal with it.

Except when it came from his daughter, he discovered.

Lillian sent him an apologetic look. "Would you like to come along, Craig?"

One look at his daughter told him her preference, and he shook his head. "No. You two go ahead. I'll do KP."

As he cleaned up, he tried not to think too far ahead. But tomorrow night, when it would be just him and Vicki, loomed ominously. In the past, the nanny had taken care of the bedtime ritual, often long before he got home from the office. And in the morning, he was gone before his daughter woke up.

It was easier that way. Less painful.

For him anyway.

The problem was, by the time he'd realized how much he'd alienated his daughter and abdicated his responsibilities as a father, he'd had no idea how to repair the damage.

He still didn't. But he had to try. He owed it to Nicole. And Vicki. And himself.

So now, together on Nantucket, they'd sink or swim.

He tried not to even consider the possibility that it would be the former.

"She's all settled." His mother reentered the kitchen and pulled out a mug to make a cup of tea, casting a discerning glance his way. "Don't take the rejection personally, Craig."

He stood with his back to the counter and pressed his palms flat behind him, gripping the edge. "How else am I supposed to take it?"

She slid the cup of water into the microwave and pressed a button. "She doesn't know you. It will be better when it's just the two of you."

"I wish I could believe that."

"Believe it. You were a wonderful father to Aaron. And to Vicki when she was a baby. Those skills are still there."

Craig thought about Maddie and how she'd responded to him. That was a good sign, he supposed. Except Maddie was a happy child who'd always been loved and cherished. And knew it, thanks to Kate.

Vicki, on the other hand, had no memory of a doting parent. Nicole had died when she was fourteen months old, and he'd been emotionally absent since then. She presented a far bigger challenge than Maddie.

"You seem doubtful."

At his mother's comment, Craig tightened his grip on the edge of the counter. "I am. When it comes to Vicki anyway." He shook his head. "She might be little, but she knows I haven't been there for her. She doesn't trust me. Rightfully so. And I don't know how to deal with that."

"By loving her. By being there for her from now on. By taking charge of her care instead of passing it off to a nanny. By doing exactly what you're doing right now. You'll win her over, Craig. I have every confidence that in six months you two will be the best of buddies. And I'll be praying for that."

So would he, Craig decided as they finished tidying up the kitchen and parted for the night. Because he was going to need all the help he could get to make the two of them a family.

Chapter Nine

When Edith opened her door the next night to admit them, she was wearing a headband sporting two playful daffodils that bobbed on gold coils above her head. Craig welcomed the comic relief. It had been a tense trip.

"Nice headpiece."

"Thanks. I'm getting in the mood for the Daffodil Festival. Only two weeks to go, you know. And our three million daffodils are determined to arrive on time. I checked them out myself along Milestone Road today. Pepped me right up after our long winter." She bent down to the little girl. "You must be Vicki."

Craig felt his daughter edge closer to him. No more than a hair. But he'd take it. She'd kept her distance during the entire trip, saying little, just staring at him with those big, solemn blue eyes.

He dropped down beside her, noting her firm grip on the tattered blanket she'd insisted on bringing with them. "This is Mrs. Shaw, Vicki. The lady I told you about, who's going to take care of you while I'm at work."

"And we're going to have so much fun." Edith smiled. "Do you like to make cookies?"

"I don't know how. But sometimes I helped my grandma."

"Perfect. I always need a good helper. Tomorrow we'll make chocolate chip ones. Do you like those?"

Vicki nodded.

"Good. Well, come on in. Kate and Maddie are already here."

Although he'd never been inside Edith's house, Craig wasn't surprised by the cozy early American decor. It suited the warm, welcoming manner of the owners.

But he was more interested in the red-haired woman and dark-eyed little girl who stood waiting for them in the living room. When Kate smiled at him, some of his tension dissipated.

"Now that we're all here, I have something for the girls." Edith opened a drawer in the antique sideboard along one wall and withdrew two coloring books and a pack of crayons. "Would you like to color until dinner?"

"I would." Maddie spoke up without hesitation and moved toward the older woman, giving Vicki a shy peek.

When his daughter didn't respond, Craig once again dropped to the balls of his feet beside her. "Do you like to color, Vicki?"

"Yes." She peeked at the other girl. "But I don't know her."

"I told you about Maddie on the plane, remember? Mrs. Shaw takes care of her, too. She's very nice."

When Vicki hesitated, Kate joined them, putting herself on the youngster's level, as well. "Hello, Vicki. I'm Maddie's mommy. Your daddy told me all about you and how happy he is you're coming to live with him. Maddie's been so excited. She hopes you'll be friends."

"I've never had a friend."

At Vicki's muted comment, compassion softened Kate's eyes. "Well, we're going to fix that. You'll have lots of friends here."

The little girl eased closer to Kate. "Are you the one who helped my daddy fix my new room?"

"Yes."

"It's pretty. Pink is my favorite color."

"Maddie picked it out. That's her favorite color, too." Kate looked toward her daughter and motioned her over, taking her hand as she approached. "Vicki likes pink, too, honey."

"I knew you would." Maddie moved closer. "My room isn't pink, but I have a lot of pink stuff in it. Maybe you can see it sometime. Could she, Mommy?"

"I think we could arrange that." Kate took the second coloring book from Edith. "Look at all these pretty pictures. What would you like to color, Vicki?"

The little girl tucked herself in beside Kate, watching as she turned the pages. "That one." She pointed to a picture of a family sitting on the ground, enjoying a picnic.

"I like that one, too." Maddie leaned over Kate's shoulder on the other side.

"I wish I had a family like that."

His daughter's wistful tone tugged at Craig's heart.

"Me, too. I only have a mommy. My daddy went to heaven," Maddie told Vicki.

"My mommy went to heaven," Vicki replied.

"But you have a nice daddy."

Vicki sent him a skeptical look, but before she could respond Edith herded the girls toward the kitchen table. Chester, wearing a daffodil boutonniere and a grin, took up the rear.

Standing, Craig helped Kate to her feet, cupping her elbow with one hand, the mohair of her flattering plum-colored sweater soft against his palm. "Thanks for smoothing out the intros."

"She's a darling girl."

"But too quiet."

A burst of childish laughter came from the kitchen, and Kate grinned. "I don't think that's going to last for long."

Craig shoved his hands in his pockets. "I hope not. The room was a hit, by the way. She was thrilled."

"I'm glad." She hesitated, as if debating whether to say more, then took the plunge. "Look, if there's anything I can do to help ease this transition, let me know. Being a single parent is tough under the best of circumstances, but you've got an even bigger challenge to overcome." She wiped her palms on her black slacks and folded her arms across her chest. "Anyway, I just wanted to let you know that if you ever need to talk, or to bounce ideas off someone, I'm available."

The offer took Craig off guard—and touched him in a way nothing had for a very long while. After leaving his mother behind and boarding the plane with Vicki, he'd felt more alone than he had since the tragic day that had robbed him of his family. But Kate's magnanimous gesture lessened his sense of isolation, giving him a beacon of hope to cling to if he floundered, much like a lighthouse offers a guiding light to those who are lost at sea.

"I appreciate that, Kate. I may take you up on it."

Edith returned then, and they had no chance to talk one-on-one the rest of the evening as they downed pizza and the daffodil-shaped sugar cookies the older woman had baked for the occasion. But after they all parted company for the night, he found he wasn't the only one who had been uplifted and encouraged by the get-together.

As he and Vicki headed toward his car, she, too, was more talkative and relaxed.

"I like Maddie," she said as he buckled her in.

"I do, too. She's a very nice little girl."

"Her mommy's nice, too."

"Yes, she is."

"But Maddie wishes she had a daddy. Just like I wish I had a mommy. Why do mommies and daddies have to die?"

Blindsided by the question, Craig secured the clip on her safety harness, glad the shadows in the car hid his face. He wished he had a good answer. But he didn't. For Vicki—or himself.

"I don't know." He framed his reply with care. "Only God

knows that. I guess He wants some of them in heaven with Him sooner than we would like."

She squished her blanket in her hands, holding it close to her chest as she regarded him in the dim light. "Are you going to die?"

At her tremulous question, his stomach clenched, and he touched her small hand with a finger that wasn't quite steady.

"God decides that, Vicki. But you know what? I plan to be around for a long, long time. I want to take you to kindergarten on your first day of school. I want to help you learn how to read. And I want to go bike riding and swimming and fishing with you. How does that sound?"

"Okay." He started to back out of the car, but she grabbed the edge of his jacket. "Will you tuck me in tonight and read me a story, like Grandma always does?"

That was the sweetest request he'd ever had. "You bet. And I plan to do that every night from now on."

Stroking her hair, he eased out of the backseat and shut the door. So far, so good.

Nevertheless, he was supremely grateful for the lifeline Kate had thrown him by offering to help if problems arose.

Because he had a feeling it was only a matter of time before he found himself in deep water—and sinking fast.

Of all the rotten luck.

As Kate secured the last mooring line to a cleat on the finger pier, she surveyed the *Lucy Sue*. Thanks to Chester, the engine was purring along. The teak trim was pristine. And she'd defy anyone to find fault with the deck after her liberal applications of elbow grease.

The problem lay under the water.

After a close encounter of the expensive kind with a wayward piece of flotsam on her way back from Great Point, her propeller now had a sizable ding. Translation: a big-bucks repair.

Once the charter season kicked in, the cost wouldn't be such an issue. But with the bluefish still making their way back to Nantucket from the warmer Florida waters where they wintered, it would be four or five more weeks before there were sufficient quantities of them to interest visitors in a fishing outing.

Disgusted, she gave the hitch knot one final tug, shoved her hands into the pockets of her slicker and trudged down Straight Wharf and onto Main Street, oblivious to the steady drizzle as she debated her options.

"Kate!"

The familiar baritone voice jerked her out of her reverie, and she lifted her head. Although she hadn't run into Craig since the pizza party at Edith's four days ago, he'd made regular appearances in her thoughts.

As he waved at her from his car and slowed to a crawl, she picked up her pace.

"Sorry if I startled you." His discerning blue eyes appraised her as she drew close. "You look upset. Is everything okay?"

She lifted one shoulder. "Depends on how you define okay. I just dinged my propeller."

"How bad is it?"

"Bad enough. She's running very rough."

"What happened?"

"I hit something out by Great Point."

"Not good."

"I'll say. And my pocketbook will agree."

The rain intensified, and she flipped up the hood on her slicker. "I better run. And you're holding up traffic."

He checked his rearview mirror. "I only see one vehicle, and it's not even close. Where are you headed?"

"Home."

"Where's your car?"

"Also home. I usually walk to the wharf." A gust of wind whipped past, flapping her slicker, and she dipped her head.

"Not the best idea today. You'll get drenched. Hop in and I'll give you a lift."

"I'm used to walking in worse weather than this. Besides, I don't want to take you away from your work."

"It's not a big deal. I was going to visit the Loran station, but I'm not keen on driving all the way to 'Sconset in this weather anyway."

She didn't blame him for that. The tower for the Coast Guard's Long Range Navigation station was on a small coast road at the far eastern end of the island, a good seven miles from Nantucket town. It would be a slow, tedious trip for a newcomer—especially if fog rolled in, as it was apt to do.

Another blast of wind whipped past, and Kate capitulated to reason. "Okay. Thanks."

Circling the car, she slid in as he opened the door for her from the inside.

"Whew. This one blew in fast." She pushed back the hood of her slicker and tried to finger comb her hair, but it was hopeless. Damp weather always made her fiery locks go berserk.

She looked over at Craig to find him watching her. And the appreciative warmth in his eyes befuddled her. How could he possibly find anything in her bedraggled state to admire? Yet Mac had often worn that same expression, she recalled. That was one of the things she'd loved about him. Even on days when she'd looked a wreck, he'd always seen past the externals and loved her for what was on the inside.

Tucking her hand in her lap, she decided they both needed a distraction. "How are you doing with Vicki?"

Turning his attention back to the road, he eased the car over the uneven cobblestones at a slow crawl. "Better than I expected. She still doesn't talk much, but she's eating okay. And she loves going to Edith's. Actually, I'm glad I ran into you. I was going to call in a day or two anyway. In case you haven't noticed, she and Maddie have become fast friends."

Kate smiled. "I've noticed. That's all Maddie talks about. It's 'Vicki and I did this,' and 'Vicki said that,' and 'why can't Vicki stay for dinner?'"

"Yeah. I've heard the same things. Since this is her first weekend here, I thought it might help to set up a playdate. I must confess I haven't a clue how to keep her entertained for two whole days on my own."

"You don't have to entertain children every minute."

"I know. But I want to be fully engaged with her until she settles in. Anyway, if it would be okay, I thought I could take them both home with me after church and drop Maddie off at your house later in the afternoon."

"Sure. That would work. And if you don't have dinner plans for that night, why don't you stay and eat with us?"

Kate had no idea why that invitation had popped out of her mouth. Judging by his arched eyebrows, neither did Craig.

But it didn't stop him from accepting. Fast. Before she could think of a way to retract it.

"That would be great. I'm trying to put some variety in our menu, but I've existed on frozen dinners for so long that any kitchen skills I once had are long gone. Macaroni and cheese pushes my abilities to the limit. And I think Vicki will get tired of that pretty quick. We've had it twice already."

Chuckling, Kate brushed a drop of rain off her forehead. "I'm not promising a gourmet dinner, but I can guarantee it won't be macaroni and cheese."

"Sold."

As he pulled up in front of her house, Kate reached for the handle of the door. Memories of the last time he'd driven her home in the rain were fresh enough in her mind to jolt her pulse into fast-forward.

"Let me get that for you." He started to open his own door.

"No!" Kate shoved her door open with more force than necessary, aware of the thread of panic that wove through her voice—and hoping he wasn't. "No sense you getting wet, too. Thanks for the ride." She slid out, bracing herself as a gust of wind buffeted her. "I'll see you Sunday."

With that she shut the door and dashed for the house. Without looking back, she fumbled for her key. Slipped it in the lock. Stepped inside. Slowly let out the breath she hadn't realized she'd been holding.

This was ridiculous.

She was acting like a schoolgirl with her first crush.

Irritated, she strode into the living room. Maddie was waiting to be retrieved, but first she needed to calm down.

Flopping into the overstuffed, chintz-covered chair, she let her head drop to the cushioned back as she sought solace in the painting above the mantel. Usually, the serenity of the timeless, windswept moors and distant sea in the scene seeped into her soul.

But not today.

Nor was she soothed by the ticking of the clock that had belonged to Mac's great-grandfather. The antique piece had sat on this mantel for more than forty years, placed there the day Mac's parents moved into this house. And when she and Mac had inherited it eight years ago, after Mac's father died, they hadn't considered moving it. To her, it had always represented roots and stability and permanence.

All the things Kate was trying so hard to hang on to in the face of her financial challenges.

But if her material security was at risk, so, too, was her emotional well-being, she acknowledged.

Thanks to Craig Cole.

In three weeks, he'd managed to turn her world upside down by reminding her what it felt like to be a woman, not just a mom. By forcing her to confront the deep-seated loneliness that had drained much of the joy from her life. By making her yearn for things she'd never expected to have again. Companionship. Partnership. Love.

Yet none of that made sense. She still loved Mac with every fiber of her being. She still felt connected to him, missed him. How was it possible to have such strong feelings for Craig? Especially when she'd known him less than a month?

Even more important, how could she have strong feelings for *any* man? Having loved and lost once, she'd vowed never to take that risk again. And she'd never been tempted to break that pledge.

Until now.

But Craig wasn't interested anyway, she reminded herself. He'd been clear on that point. Romance wasn't on his agenda.

And even if, over time, they finally both felt comfortable exploring a relationship, one other looming hurdle stood in Kate's path.

Fear.

She'd learned with Mac that giving your heart carried a sizable risk. When he'd been taken from her, she'd wanted to die, too. Maddie had given her a reason to carry on, but without her daughter's needs to attend to, pushing her to get up every day and go through the motions of life, there was a good chance she would have succumbed to the blackness that had been sucking her down to a place she never, ever wanted to go again. A place from which even her strong faith hadn't been able to protect her.

She might not want to live the rest of her life alone, Kate reflected as she rose to retrieve Maddie. But neither did she want to risk another devastating loss.

And that was a stumbling block she doubted she would ever overcome.

Chapter Ten

"Okay. Now cross your fingers and let's see if we can add one more to top off this fabulous castle." As the two little girls seated on the living room floor beside him watched, Craig added a final block to the tower.

The column wavered. The girls gasped. It steadied. They sighed.

"Wow. That's the tallest castle I've ever built," Maddie said in awe.

"Yeah," Vicki seconded.

As the phone began to ring, Craig carefully extricated himself from the pile of blocks around him. "You girls can build the wall around it while I answer that."

They set about the task with vigor, and he smiled. He'd been worried all week about how to entertain the two of them for several hours, but as he'd discovered, their active imaginations took care of that problem.

Striding across the kitchen, he picked up the phone, wondering if Kate was calling to check in. He wouldn't mind hearing her voice about now, he decided, his smile widening.

But the woman's voice that greeted him on the other end didn't belong to the charter fishing captain.

"Hi, Mom. Is everything okay?" It was always the first thing he asked when she called, though by now it had become perfunctory. For a while after his dad died seven years ago, he'd worried about his mother living alone in the house his parents had shared for thirty-five years. But Lillian Cole had done fine, proving far more capable of managing her solo life than he'd expected.

"Right as rain. How's everything going there?"

"Not bad. So far."

Childish giggles erupted from the living room, followed by the sound of tumbling blocks. So much for his castle, he thought with a grin.

"Do I hear children?"

"Good ears, Mom."

"I may be old, but all the parts still work. Does Vicki have a playmate?"

"It's the other little girl from the day care situation I arranged. They've gotten to be great friends already."

"Good. That's just what she needs. A companion her own age. And speaking of companions…I have some exciting news. Brace yourself—I'm getting married."

Craig was shocked into silence.

"I got sort of the same reaction from your brother."

At Lillian's amused comment, Craig located his voice. "Why didn't you tell me last week, when I was there?"

"Because he just proposed last night."

"I assume Harold is the groom?"

"Who else? He's a good man, Craig. You'll like him once you get to know him better."

"I already like him, Mom." Harold Simmons, with his shock of white hair and British accent, had impressed Craig as a true gentleman. A year ago, at seventy-two, he'd moved into Craig's hometown to be near his daughter and grandchildren. Bored after three months, he'd proceeded to purchase a small local book store, declaring he'd found his true calling. Better late than never, he'd told Craig with a wink at Christmas. And providential, too, as he'd pointed out, because that was how he'd met Lillian. She'd gone in to buy a book, ended up staying for tea—and the rest had been history.

"So when's the wedding?" he asked.

"That's the next thing I wanted to talk to you about. Harold and I would like to be married next month. On Nantucket. I've heard it's a beautiful place, and with you there and Steve in New York, it would be a convenient location for our family. And Harold's daughter doesn't mind traveling there for the ceremony. She says it would be a good excuse for a vacation."

"You're not wasting any time, are you?"

"At our age, there's not much time to waste. Why wait?"

"Good point. What can I do to help?"

"Shall I read you my whole list now, or give it to you in small chunks?"

At her teasing tone, he laughed. "Hit me with all of it."

"Okay. Let's start with the minister. Can you recommend someone?"

"You'd like the pastor at the church I'm attending, and I'm sure he'd be happy to perform the ceremony. The church itself is nice, too."

"To be honest, Harold and I would prefer to get married in a natural setting. We both did the big church wedding the first time around. And I figure the Lord will be with us whether we're in His house or His backyard."

Craig smiled. "That sounds fine to me."

"We also want to arrange a small, simple reception. And Harold and I will need somewhere to stay for a week. I hoped you might be able to recommend someone familiar with the island who could help me pull all the pieces together."

Kate came to mind at once, but Craig quickly discarded that notion. She might know all the ins and outs of the island, but she was also a single mom with two seasonal jobs who didn't have a minute to call her own as it was.

"I'll give it some thought, Mom. Let me talk to Reverend Kaizer and I'll get back to you later in the week. What day did you have in mind for the ceremony?"

"We were hoping for Monday, May twenty-second. That way, we could all fly in over the weekend and get settled. And Monday should be a quieter day on the island. Given the short notice, that should open a few more options in terms of venues."

"True." Craig jotted down the date. "Anything else?"

"Isn't that enough for one day?"

He grinned. "Yeah, it is. Okay, I'll be back in touch soon. And Mom…I'm really happy for you."

"Thank you, dear. To be honest, the whole thing took me by surprise, too. I thought my life was fine as it was. But in hindsight, it was like the days I work late in my garden, not even noticing how dim the world has grown until I step inside, flip on a light and realize I'd been in the shadows. That's what Harold did for me, Craig. He flipped on the light in my life again."

Craig's throat constricted. "I'm happy you found someone new to love, Mom."

"I thank the Lord for that great blessing every day. And it might interest you to know that while I have His ear I also pray He blesses you with a second chance at love."

Once again, an image of Kate flashed through Craig's mind. And once again, he stifled it.

"I appreciate the thought, Mom. But don't hold your breath. I'm not planning another foray into matrimony."

"I wasn't, either. It was God's idea. And His plans don't always mesh with ours, as I discovered. Just be open to them, son. And don't rule anything out."

His mother's words resonating in his ear, Craig said goodbye and ambled back to the living room. The two little girls were engrossed in their make-believe castle game, creating worlds where heroic knights on white chargers slew dragons and lived happily ever after with the fair maidens they rescued. No shadows darkened their idyllic existence.

But there were plenty of shadows in real life. And heroes tended to have feet of clay.

Still, Craig couldn't help wishing the Lord would hear his mother's prayers and help him find a way to give his own life a happily ever after.

"That was the bestest chocolate cake I ever ate." Vicki swiped at her mouth with a paper napkin, managing to smear the icing rather than remove it.

"I second that." Craig grinned and leaned over to wipe the excess off her chin.

"The spaghetti was good, too," Maddie chimed in.

"I second that, as well." Craig took a sip of coffee and sent Kate a warm smile that turned her insides to mush.

Rising, she began to clear the table.

"Let me help."

Before she could protest, Craig stood, too, and picked up the girls' plates.

"Mommy, can me and Vicki play in my room?"

"Sure."

The two girls scampered off.

As Kate led the way into the small kitchen, the youngsters' chatter drifted down the hall from Maddie's room.

"She had a good time." Craig paused in the doorway, listening. "I haven't managed to elicit that kind of response from her yet."

His wistful tone tugged at Kate's heart. "Give her time."

"You sound like my mother." He sent her a grin that looked forced. "I had some surprising news from her today, by the way. She called to say—"

A knock sounded at Kate's back door, and she wiped her hands on a dish towel as she moved toward it. "Don't lose your train of thought."

"Sorry to bother you when you have company, Kate." Edith peered over her neighbor's shoulder as Kate opened the door and waved at Craig. "But this came for you yesterday while you were out and Chester forgot to bring it over. I had a feeling you might be waiting for it." She handed Kate an overnight package.

"Thanks. I was." Kate took the bulky envelope and set it on the kitchen table.

Edith followed her in. No surprise there, Kate reflected. She'd probably been delighted to have an excuse to scope out the dinner party next door.

"I hope I didn't interrupt anything." Edith gave Kate and Craig a hopeful look.

"No. We were just clearing the table." Craig set down the plates he was balancing. "And I was getting ready to share some news with Kate."

"Oh?" Edith's expression changed from hopeful to curious.

"I had a call from my mother this afternoon. She's getting married."

"A wedding!" Edith perked up. "Isn't that romantic?"

Craig grinned. "I guess so. But it's hard to think about my mom in that light."

"I'll have you know that romance knows no age limits, young man," Edith chided him. "When's the big day?"

"She's hoping for May twenty-second. And they want to have the wedding here. Preferably outdoors. I'm supposed to arrange things with Reverend Kaizer."

"What about a reception?"

"I'm supposed to find someone to arrange that, too."

"Hmm." Edith cocked her head. "Will this be a small wedding?"

"Very. No more than fifteen people."

"I'll tell you what, Craig. If you think your mother would be interested, I'd be happy to coordinate things on this end."

Kate gave her a suspicious look. Edith ignored it.

"Are you serious?" Craig stared at her. "Despite the small size, it will still be a lot of work."

She waved his comment aside. "I don't mind in the least. Why don't you discuss it with your mother, and if she's agreeable have her give me a call."

"I'll do that. And thank you."

"My pleasure." She checked her watch. "Gotta run. There's a program on public TV tonight that Chester and I want to catch. Enjoy your evening." She hustled through the door, pulling it shut behind her.

"Wow." Craig shook his head. "Is she always such a go-getter?"

"Yes." Especially when she's on a mission, Kate thought, though she left that unsaid. But whatever Edith's hidden agenda, the truth was she'd do a good job for Craig's mother. "She's great at coordinating events. She's a past president of the garden club, and under her supervision we had some of the best Daffodil Festivals ever. Plus, she knows everybody on the island. Count your blessings for the offer."

"I'm counting my blessings on a lot of fronts these days."

His comment, rife with personal implications, and the soft light in his eyes sent warmth coursing through her. Turning away, Kate busied herself wiping down the counter.

"I'll go check on the girls," he offered.

"Good idea."

Get a grip, Kate admonished herself as she tried to rein in her overactive imagination. She had to be reading way too much into his remark. Hadn't he told her he had no interest in romance? Hadn't she told him the same thing?

Yet try as she might, she couldn't stifle the tiny flame of hope that flickered to life in her heart.

Craig didn't hurry back to the kitchen. Instead, he gave in to Maddie's plea to read the girls a story. He needed some space from the lovely woman who was fast undermining his conviction that he didn't deserve a second chance at love. Life felt brighter and more vibrant when he was with her. In her presence, the shadows his mother had talked about lightened.

But even if he could get past the guilt, the situation with Kate was complicated. She earned her living on the sea. The same sea that had robbed him of his wife and son. A relationship with her would carry risks. Big risks. Wouldn't it be testing fate to take that kind of chance?

Yet now that she had roused from hibernation the happy memories of his fulfilling marriage, how would he ever find the strength to cope with the endless parade of solitary months and years stretching ahead?

"You have to read the last line, Lootenin. That's the best part."

At Maddie's comment, Craig refocused his attention on the book in his hands. The last line was the standard fairy-tale ending.

"And they lived happily ever after."

The words sounded hollow to his ears. Maybe that's why he'd hesitated. Much as he yearned for one of his own, in his experience happy endings were the stuff of dreams, not reality.

"Will you read us another one, Lootenin?"

At Maddie's question, he shook his head. "Not tonight. Vicki and I have to go home now."

"Can't we stay longer?" Vicki pleaded. "I like it here."

So did he, Craig agreed. "You'll see Maddie tomorrow, at Mrs. Shaw's."

"Okay, I guess." She crawled across Maddie's bed and slid

off, reaching for the tattered blanket that was never more than an arm's length away.

Taking her hand, Craig led her down the hall, Maddie trailing at their heels.

When they reached the kitchen doorway, Kate turned to them. For an instant he thought he saw disappointment in her eyes. But she quickly masked it.

"Heading home?"

"Yes. Thank you for a wonderful dinner."

"Thank you for arranging the playdate. It gave me a chance to get a lot of work done."

From the way she said work, he got the impression she wasn't talking about housecleaning or laundry.

"Did you go down to the *Lucy Sue?*"

"No." She gestured to the package Edith had delivered. "In my spare time I do freelance book editing for a publisher in New York. A friend of mine had a connection there and got me in. It'll never make me rich, but it's a nice supplement to my income and the hours are flexible. I work on the manuscripts at night, after Maddie's in bed."

So Kate had *three* jobs.

As he processed this new piece of information, Craig recalled her telling him once that despite the financial pressures she faced, she intended to stay on the island. And it was obvious she was doing everything humanly possible to make that happen.

Early in their relationship, Craig had concluded Kate was strong. But she was more than strong, he now realized. She was a survivor. The kind of woman who might get discouraged but who would keep fighting until every last piece of ammunition was gone.

"You're amazing."

Her eyes widened, and a faint, becoming blush stained her cheeks. But she sidestepped his compliment. "Stubborn is more like it."

"I stand by my first comment. But I do have one question. When do you sleep?"

Her blush deepened. "Quality is more important than quantity. And I sleep better knowing I'm solvent."

"What's solvent?"

At Maddie's question, Kate shot her daughter a surprised glance, as if she'd forgotten there was an audience to their conversation. Truth be told, he, too, had forgotten the presence of the children as he focused on the extraordinary woman across from him.

"It means different things for different people, honey. For me, it means happy."

"Oh. I guess I'm solvent, too, then."

Craig grinned, and Kate smiled back. "Let me get your coats."

After retrieving them, she helped Vicki zip hers up while Craig slid his arms into his leather jacket. Opening the door, Kate stepped back, one hand still on the knob, the other resting on Maddie's shoulder. "Looks like it's going to rain again. Drive safe."

Go! Just say good-night and go! The compelling command echoed in Craig's mind. And he knew he should listen to it.

But Kate looked so appealing. The golden light on the hall table spilled across her cheeks, warming her skin and gilding her hair. And how could he ignore the soft, unspoken invitation in her emerald eyes, the one he suspected she wasn't even aware of? Or the call of her satiny smooth skin?

In the end, he couldn't.

Leaning close, he brushed his lips against the gentle curve of her cheek. Lingered. Drew back.

"Good night, Kate."

She didn't respond.

Taking Vicki's hand, he led the little girl into the night and toward his car, shaken by the step he'd just taken.

To an onlooker, the kiss would have appeared to be

innocent. Casual. The kind often exchanged by mere ac-
quaintances.

But for them, he sensed it had been a prelude.

A dip of the toes to test the water.

Kate had been startled by his touch. Too startled to react.
He'd have to wait until they next met to get a read on how
she viewed it.

As for his own reaction—it had been anything but casual.

Because that simple touch of lips to cheek had left him
wanting more.

And he had no idea what to do about that.

Later, long after Maddie had been tucked in for the night,
long after Kate should have been asleep, she lay wide awake,
staring at the ceiling in her room. Remembering the touch of
Craig's lips against her cheek.

Lifting her hand, she pressed her fingers to the spot. Drew
in a long, slow breath.

But the calming technique did nothing to quiet her restless-
ness.

Shoving the covers back, she swung her feet to the floor,
grabbed her robe and padded down the hall toward the living
room. After flipping on a light, she tucked her legs under her
on the sofa and focused on Mac's painting, letting its quiet
beauty seep into her soul.

As usual, she found herself appreciating anew the sensi-
tive rendering that reflected the soul of a man in love with life.
A man who'd been able to find beauty in unexpected places
and whose masterful talent had allowed others to see the
world as he saw it. A man who'd always seized opportunities
for joy, who'd believed in the heart's infinite capacity to love.

Of all people, Mac would understand that nothing could
ever diminish what they'd shared. The man who'd stolen her
heart and filled her days with sunshine and beauty and grace,

who'd taught her that life was to be embraced, would understand that the part of herself she'd given to him would be his, and his alone, for always. And he would want her to move on. To love again if the opportunity came along.

She knew that now.

Yet the fear of loving—and losing—remained. While Craig appeared to be healthy and vibrant, Mac had exuded vigor, too. Yet, as Kate had learned, life didn't come with guarantees—at any age. And she didn't know if she could live with that constant worry.

As she wrestled with indecision, the clock on the mantel began to intone the hour. She listened as twelve steady, predictable bongs echoed in the quiet room. A room where she ended each day the same way.

Alone.

And lonely.

But perhaps God was offering her an opportunity to change that if she could find the courage to open herself to love. To encourage the interest Craig had displayed tonight.

Kate's instincts pushed her toward self-preservation. Yet her parched heart yearned for love, much as the plants in her garden needed the restoring rain the approaching storm would bring.

It was a dilemma for which she had no answer.

Rising wearily, Kate took one more look at the painting before she returned to bed. And sent a short, silent plea heavenward.

Lord, please guide me as I struggle to determine Your will for me. Don't let fear hold me back…but don't let my own needs and loneliness cloud my judgment, either. And give me the courage to put fear aside and claim the future You have planned for me—whatever it may be.

Chapter Eleven

Craig emptied his pockets of change and set the coins on the dresser in his room, stifling a yawn. It had been a hectic, crisis-filled day at the station, leaving him tired and on edge. And things at home had been stressful, too. Vicki had picked at her dinner, balked at taking a bath and turned thumbs down on all the books he'd suggested as a bedtime story.

Missing her nap today hadn't helped her disposition, he supposed. But thanks to the asthma attack Maddie had suffered, the girls' routine had been disrupted. Edith had told him about it when he'd picked up Vicki, warning him she'd been upset by the incident. During the evening he'd tried to get his daughter to talk about it, but she'd wanted nothing to do with the subject, closing up as tight as a Nantucket quahog when he broached the topic.

Picking up the photo on his dresser, he ran a finger over the smooth koa-wood frame, a familiar pang echoing in his heart as memories of happier times surfaced. He'd always loved this family picture, a casual four-by-six snapshot taken on a weekend trip to Volcanoes National Park on the Big Island a couple of years before the tragic accident. The dramatic, black lava rock had provided the perfect backdrop for their laughing, animated faces, offering a sharp contrast to Aaron's light brown hair and Nicole's long, wavy blond mane.

The sudden pressure of tears behind his eyes surprised him. It had been a long time since he'd gotten emotional over the events that had upended his world, and the unexpected loss of control threw him. *Get a grip,* he admonished himself. *This is history. You need to—*

"Daddy?"

At Vicki's soft question, he jerked toward her. She was standing two feet away, clutching an empty plastic cup, her ratty blanket trailing behind her.

Swallowing past the lump in his throat, he returned the photo to the dresser. "Do you need some water?"

She nodded.

"Coming right up." He took the cup from her hand.

She didn't follow him to the kitchen, as he expected. And when he headed back down the hall, thinking she'd returned to bed, he stopped short when he found her still in his room, her back to the door, contemplating the photo on his dresser.

"I have your water, Vicki. You can drink it in your room."

She spoke without turning. "Where's me?"

Her plaintive, forlorn question twisted his gut.

Setting the glass on the chest next to the door, he moved beside her. "That was taken before you were born, honey."

A few seconds of silence ticked by as she inspected it. "Is that my mommy?"

"Yes. And that's Aaron, your brother."

She looked up at him. "How come the picture makes you sad?"

Apparently she'd been standing there watching him longer than he'd thought, Craig concluded. "Because I miss them."

"Would you miss me if I was gone?"

At her wistful tone, the pressure once more built behind his eyes. "Of course I would."

She turned again to the picture. "But how would you remember me?"

For such a tiny thing, she sure knew how to rip the heart right out of him.

"You're right. I need some more pictures. I'll tell you what. Tomorrow, on my lunch hour, I'm going to buy a camera so I can take pictures of us together. Would you like that?"

She examined the photo again. Rather than answer his question, she asked another of her own. "Do you think my mommy was pretty?"

Craig tried to stop the tears from welling in his eyes, but it was a losing battle as he knelt beside his daughter. "She was beautiful, honey." His words came out raspy. Raw. He cleared his throat. "Just like you are. In fact, your hair is exactly the same color as hers was. It makes me think of your mommy."

She gave him the solemn look that always made him wonder what was going on in her little mind. He braced for more questions, but to his surprise she edged around him and walked toward the door. "Can I have my water now?"

"Sure." He rose and picked up the glass off the dresser. When he handed it to her, she took a long drink and passed it back. Without a word, she traipsed back down the hall toward her room, trailing her blanket behind her.

He followed, sensing he was missing some important cue, but for the life of him he didn't know what it was. Or how to figure it out.

"How about that story now?" He fiddled with the covers as she climbed into bed, delaying his departure. Despite the late hour, he felt the need to be close to her.

"No, thank you." She tucked the blanket under her chin, snuggled under the covers and closed her eyes.

He'd been dismissed.

Baffled, Craig retreated to his own room. Moving to the window, he shoved his hands in his pockets. Ominous clouds had begun to mass at sunset, and now the moon and stars were hidden behind a black mantle. A threat of rain hung in the air, and a pervasive chill had settled over the island.

The unsettled weather matched his mood—and he didn't know why. Vicki appeared to be calm. There'd been no tears. No tantrums. No displays of temper.

Yet he couldn't help feeling that somehow he'd just made a big mistake.

Three days had passed since their spaghetti dinner with the girls, and Kate was still trying to interpret the look in Craig's eye and the kiss he'd dropped on her cheek as they'd parted.

More importantly, she was still struggling to come to grips with her own reaction. And until she got a handle on her feelings, she'd decided to cut a wide swath around the handsome lieutenant.

But tonight was dicey. She'd been delayed at school, attending another endless faculty meeting. Craig's car wasn't in front of Edith's house when she pulled onto Lighthouse Lane, but he could arrive any second. She needed to get Maddie ASAP and make a fast retreat.

Parking her car, she headed straight for Edith's back door. But Chester waylaid her in the yard.

"Afternoon, Kate. Do you have a minute?"

Casting a wishful look at the back door, Kate veered off the path toward the older man, who was at last putting the finishing touches on the guest cottage. "What's up, Chester?"

"Would you mind holding this door knocker in place while I screw it on? It'll only take a minute, and I could use another pair of hands. Edith's been too busy with the girls to help me out today."

"Sure."

The one minute stretched to five, with Kate growing more

antsy by the second. When at last Chester stepped back and pronounced the job done, she took off at a trot for the door. "Gotta run, Chester. It's looking good."

"Thanks." He acknowledged her compliment with a wave and went back to work.

Edith opened the door before she even knocked, greeting her with a grin. "I see Chester put you to work."

"He needed another set of hands." She tried not to sound anxious. "Sorry for the delay today."

"No problem." The other woman cocked her head. "Are you in a rush?"

"Yes. Lots to do tonight. Is Maddie ready?"

"The girls have been engrossed in a puzzle, and I didn't want to disturb them until you got here. Come on in and I'll get her jacket."

Kate followed her into the kitchen. In the adjacent sunroom, Maddie and Vicki were kneeling on their chairs, elbows on the glass-topped wrought iron table, fitting over-size puzzle pieces together.

"Here we go." Edith reentered the kitchen. "Maddie, your mommy's here."

The little girl frowned. "But we're almost done."

"You can finish it tomorrow, honey," Kate told her. "Mommy's got a lot to do tonight."

Heaving a loud sigh, Maddie made a project out of climbing down off her chair, then trudged into the kitchen, dragging her feet.

To Kate, she appeared to be moving in slow motion.

Reining in her impatience, she tried to appear calm and un-ruffled. But not much got past Edith's eagle eye.

"You seem on edge, Kate. Everything okay?"

"Sure. Fine. Come on, Maddie, we need to go."

Just as Maddie reached her, the doorbell rang.

Edith brightened. "That must be Craig. I'll be right back."

Before Kate could respond, she trotted toward the living room.

Hustling Maddie into her coat, Kate grabbed her hand and headed toward the back door.

"Wait, Mommy." Maddie hung back. "Aren't we going to say hello to the lootenin?"

"Not today. I'm in a hurry."

As she gave Maddie's arm a gentle tug, a yelp came from the sunroom, followed by a clatter. Dropping Maddie's hand, Kate switched directions and dashed toward the ominous noise.

She found Vicki on the floor, fat tears oozing out her eyes, her chair overturned beside her.

Dropping to one knee, Kate smoothed back her hair and took a quick inventory as she spoke. "What happened, sweetie?"

"It t-tipped over when I t-tried to slide off."

"Does anything hurt?"

The little girl shook her head. "No, but it s-scared me."

Helping the little girl up, Kate did one more inspection. "It would scare me, too. But you're fine now."

"What's the problem?"

In her concern for the little girl, Kate hadn't heard Craig approach. Now, as he dropped beside her, the faint, masculine scent of his aftershave invaded her senses. And when she looked into his blue eyes, mere inches way, they sucked her in like a relentless tide, leaving her floundering.

"The chair tipped. She's fine." Her words came out breathless. She hoped he wouldn't notice.

He maintained eye contact for a moment longer than necessary, and a tiny flame sparked to life in those baby blues.

He'd noticed.

"Thanks for coming to the rescue."

She adopted a bright tone. "All in a day's work." Rising, she moved away, anxious to put some distance between them.

To her relief, he stayed at Vicki's level for a few more seconds.

"Are you sure you're okay, honey?" He reached out and tucked his daughter's hair behind her ear.

She sniffled again and nodded.

"We'll finish the puzzle tomorrow, okay, Vicki?" Maddie moved in closer and gave her friend's shoulder a consoling pat.

"Okay."

"Well. That's enough excitement for one day." Edith stepped forward and handed Vicki's jacket to Craig.

Maddie watched as he helped his daughter slide her arms through. "Are you going to kiss Mommy goodbye again?"

Kate wanted to sink through the floor.

And the flush on the back of Craig's neck told her he was equally embarrassed.

She didn't even want to look at Edith.

Keeping his head averted, Craig buttoned Vicki's jacket. Very slowly. "That was a thank-you for such a nice meal. What was your favorite part of the dinner, Vicki?"

"The chocolate cake."

Craig finished buttoning her coat and stood. "Me, too. And Mrs. Shaw is a good baker, too. I'll bet you had some goodies today, too, didn't you?"

"Uh-huh. Oatmeal cookies."

"We helped her bake them," Maddie added.

Smooth, Kate thought, admiring his ability to distract the girls.

"See you tomorrow, Edith." Craig took Vicki's hand. When he looked at her, Kate once more felt warmth spill onto her cheeks. "Take care, Kate. Bye, Maddie."

"Bye, Lootenin."

As Edith ushered Craig and Vicki out, Maddie inspected her. "Why is your face red, Mommy?"

No question about it, Kate decided. The diplomacy gene was missing from the MacDonald women.

"I'm getting hot standing here in my coat. We need to go."

Any hope of getting out the door before Edith returned vanished, however, when the older woman hustled back into the room. She must have pushed the other duo out the front door without ceremony, Kate concluded.

"He kissed you, hmm?"

Oh, why had she been born a redhead? Kate lamented as her face flamed again. "It was a peck on the cheek."

"Right."

"Edith." Kate tried for a stern tone. "Don't get ideas."

The woman gave her a satisfied smirk. "It would appear I'm not the only one with ideas."

Shaking her head, Kate headed toward the door. "You're hopeless."

"No." Edith followed her. "Hope*ful.*"

"I give up."

"Good. Because if you ask me, this one's a keeper."

"I'm out of here."

Taking a firm grip on Maddie's hand, Kate led the little girl out the door and down the steps.

"Mommy." Maddie tugged on her hand as they cut across the grass, heading for the gate that separated the two yards. "What's a keeper?"

"It means something you always want to have with you."

And as she eased the gate open and ushered her daughter through, Kate was forced to admit that Craig Cole seemed to fit that definition to a T.

"Sorry to interrupt, sir. But I thought you might want to take this call."

Craig looked up from the material he was reviewing to prep for the role he'd inherited on the Nantucket Shipwreck & Lifesaving Museum board. His executive petty officer stood on the threshold of his office.

"Who is it?"

"Katherine MacDonald. She said it's important."

It must be, if she was calling him after that embarrassing fiasco at Edith's yesterday, Craig decided. From the quick glance he'd aimed her direction as he and Vicki left, he'd gotten the distinct impression she hoped their paths wouldn't cross again until the next millennium.

"Okay. Put her through."

As Barlow exited, the man flashed his commanding officer a rakish grin. Craig ignored it. He had more important things to think about than his aide's slight impertinence.

Like an appealing charter captain with flashing green eyes and hair the color of glowing embers.

The phone rang, and he snatched up the receiver. "Kate? It's Craig."

"I'm sorry to bother you at work."

At the distress in her voice, a shot of adrenaline sharpened his reflexes, much as it had in his rescue-swimmer days after he'd been assigned a dangerous mission. "No problem. What's up?"

"Edith had to run to church to deal with some Daffodil Festival–related catastrophe, and since I'm not subbing today she asked if I could bring Maddie over this afternoon and watch Vicki while she was gone. I'm at her house now. But a situation has come up I think you may want to deal with."

"Is Vicki hurt?" He tightened his grip on the phone.

"No. Nothing like that." Her volume dropped. "I was working on a manuscript and I thought the girls were doing another puzzle in the sunroom. But they got very quiet after a while, and when I went in there I discovered they'd taken the scissors to Vicki's hair. And they were trying to color what was left with markers. I can't get any explanation out of either of them. But it's…a mess."

"I can be there in less than ten minutes. Hang tight."

Ending the call, Craig stuffed the Lifesaving Museum material into his briefcase, told Barlow he was leaving for the day and drove to Edith's house as fast as the bone-jarring cobblestones would allow.

As Kate had warned him, Vicki was a wreck. When he entered the sunroom, the two little girls were huddled together on one chair, their hands stained with black streaks. They hung their heads when he appeared, giving him a good view of the chop job they'd done on Vicki's hair. Tufts of varying lengths stuck out in all directions, and they'd tried to color what little was left with a black marker.

Craig had no idea what to make of it. Based on her bewildered shrug, neither did Kate.

One thing he knew—neither little girl was prone to mischief. There had to be a reason for this…if he could ferret it out. And if he did get an explanation, his gut told him that the way he handled the situation was going to have a huge impact on his relationship with his daughter.

Praying he'd say and do the right things, Craig crossed the room and dropped to the balls of his feet in front of the two little girls. He sensed Kate hovering in the background and took comfort in her presence. If he got into trouble, it was good to know there was an experienced reinforcement close by.

"Hey." He kept his tone gentle and reached for their small hands. "We're going to fix this."

Maddie peeked up at him first. "Are you mad?"

"Were you being naughty?"

"No. We were trying to make everything better."

The explanation was incomprehensible to him. But it seemed to make sense to the two girls.

"It wasn't Maddie's fault." Vicki raised her chin. It started to quiver. "She only cut the back. I asked her to because I couldn't reach it."

"Was this your idea, Vicki?"

The little girl nodded.

"Maddie, let's go wash your hands." Kate moved into the

room, waiting as Maddie slid off the chair before directing her next comment to Craig. "We'll be down the hall. Close by if you need us."

He telegraphed a silent *thank-you* with his eyes.

As mother and daughter disappeared, Vicki's chin continued to quiver. Following his instincts, Craig lifted her off the chair and folded her in his arms, tucking her head against his shoulder as he stood. He tried to recall the last time he'd held her like this. Couldn't.

But it felt good. And right.

"Hey." He stroked what little was left of her hair. "It's okay, Vicki. I know you had a reason for doing this. If we sit together in that big chair in Mrs. Shaw's living room, will you tell me about it?"

A sniffle was her only response.

Choosing to interpret that as a yes, he walked into the next room and eased into the wing chair, tucking her into the crook of his arm as he settled her on his lap.

They remained like that for a full minute, but when Vicki didn't speak, Craig took the initiative. "Didn't you like your long hair anymore, honey?"

She shook her head, leaving it burrowed on his chest.

He fingered the short, stubby locks and a pang echoed in his heart. "You had such pretty hair. Just like your mommy's."

"I don't want to be like Mommy."

The fierceness of her response startled him. "Why not?"

"Because when you look at her picture you're sad. I don't want you to be sad when you look at me. I thought if I changed how I looked, you might be h-happier when you're with m-me."

Her sobbed response ripped his gut. And left him feeling raw inside. Incompetent. And unworthy.

But he wasn't going to give up.

Swallowing past the lump in his throat, Craig smoothed the hair back from his daughter's forehead. "I'm not sad when I look at you, Vicki. Because I love what's in here," he touched her chest, above her heart, "more than what's up here." He stroked her hair again. "I love you for who you are. Sometimes people look alike, like you and your mommy, but every single person in the whole world is different. There's nobody else just like you, and there never will be. You're special. And I love you for that. For being my special little girl. No matter what color your hair is."

He shifted her around so she could better see into his eyes. "When your mommy and brother went to heaven, I was very sad. And for a long time I forgot about everything else. I'm sorry about that now. I wish I could start over with you from the very beginning. But I promise, from now on I'm not going to think about yesterday anymore. I'm going to think about tomorrow, and all the fun we're going to have together."

She studied him, with eyes he would never again let himself think of as Nicole's but as Vicki's. He endured her solemn scrutiny, praying his words had found their way into her heart.

Reaching out, she laid her palm against his cheek. "Promise?"

"Promise." His voice choked, and he cleared his throat. "In fact, let's do something fun tonight. I know—how would you like to have chocolate chip waffles for dinner?"

Her face lit up. "I've never had those."

"Me, neither. But we'll figure out how to make them together."

Holding her close, he rose, turned—and found Kate staring at him with a stunned expression.

"Kate?"

She blinked. "Maddie and I are heading home."

"So are we." He gestured toward Vicki's hair. "Any suggestions on how to remedy this?"

She blinked again. Gave him a distracted look. "My hairdresser is very good. And she works late on Thursdays. I could give her a call and see if she can squeeze in an emergency."

"I'd appreciate it."

"Give me a minute."

As she disappeared into Edith's kitchen, Maddie edged closer. "Mommy says we can make daffy hats tomorrow, Vicki."

His daughter looked down at her friend but didn't loosen her grip around his neck. And that suited him fine. "Okay."

"What's a daffy hat?" Craig asked.

"It's a hat decorated with daffodils," Maddie told him. "For the festival on Saturday. You're going, aren't you?"

Vicki edged back so she could see his face. "We are, aren't we, Daddy?"

The town was buzzing with festival preparations, but Craig hadn't thought much about it. The Coast Guard always hung a daffodil wreath on tiny Brant Point Light, but other than that he had no official involvement. And he'd been too busy to make any personal plans for the event.

"I guess we can. I'll have to find out a little more about it."

"It's lots of fun," Maddie said. "Isn't it, Mommy?"

Kate had reappeared in the doorway, holding a slip of paper. "What is, honey?"

"The Daffodil Festival."

"Oh, yes. Lots of fun." She crossed the room and passed him the information. "I jotted down the address. Just ask for Chloe when you get there. She'll be expecting you."

"Can Vicki and the lootenin go to the parade with us, Mommy? I told him we were going to make hats tomorrow."

Kate turned to him. "Were you planning to go?"

"I didn't have plans one way or the other. What's the story on the hats?"

"A lot of people decorate hats to wear for the Daffy Hat Pageant. Mostly tourists, to be honest. But I thought the girls would get a kick out of it." She tucked a springy lock of hair behind her ear. "If the weather's good, Maddie and I are going to watch the antique car parade on Main Street. You're welcome to join us, if you like."

The invitation took him off guard. He'd assumed their impromptu kiss would send her running in the opposite direction. Instead, she was suggesting another get-together. Was empathy for Vicki the reason? Or was she opening a door for the two of them?

Craig didn't have the answers to those questions. All he knew was that if he wanted to stick by his vow to remain unattached, accepting would not be a smart idea.

As he opened his mouth to decline, Vicki spoke.

"Could we, Daddy? Please? It would be fun."

He was sunk. He knew it the second he looked into those hopeful blue-green eyes inches from his. And once more scanned her shorn hair.

"I guess we can. Give me a time and place to meet."

Kate filled him in on the details, and five minutes later he and Vicki were on their way to see Chloe.

But as they drove through the narrow streets, Craig couldn't help thinking that attending a pleasant, social event in the company of the appealing charter captain and her charming daughter wasn't going to do a thing to neutralize the chemistry between them. Just the opposite.

Yet, for the first time, he didn't feel a rush of panic at that thought. Thanks to a lot of prayer in recent weeks, he was reconnecting with the Lord and beginning to accept that God had forgiven him for whatever role he'd played in the tragedy that had taken his family. Although he wasn't ready to be that generous with himself, he was getting close to finding the strength to let it go and move on.

Kate's connection to the sea—and the risk that carried—was still a stumbling block, however.

Yet if he ever did reach the point where he felt ready to open his heart to love, he could think of no finer woman to woo than Kate MacDonald.

Chapter Twelve

"There he is, Mommy!"

At Maddie's excited comment, Kate followed the direction of her daughter's finger. In seconds she spotted Craig on the other side of the street, wearing khaki slacks and a chest-hugging golf shirt that revealed impressive biceps. Vicki was hidden by the legs of spectators lined up on Main Street for the parade, but she caught a quick glimpse of blond hair. Good. Chloe had at least managed to get rid of the dye from the marker.

"Mommy, aren't you going to wave at him?" Maddie tugged on her hand.

"Yes, honey. I was waiting until he looked this way."

That was only partly true. She was also waiting for her pulse to settle down after the leap it had taken the instant she'd laid eyes on him. In truth, though, she suspected the parade would be over before that happened. She'd just have to deal with the powerful effect he had on her, she told herself, lifting a hand to wave.

When he caught sight of her, he took advantage of a balky engine that left a temporary gap in the lineup of vintage vehicles. Sweeping Vicki into his arms, he strode across the cobblestone street and stepped onto the sidewalk beside them.

"Now those are what I call hats."

"We put the daffodils on them this morning," Maddie volunteered, touching the straw brim of her ribbon-and-flower-bedecked bonnet. "We found some pink ones for yours, Vicki. Show her, Mommy."

Kate knelt in front of Vicki, impressed by her hairdresser's finesse. Chloe had done a masterful job of salvaging the child's locks, giving her a wispy pixie cut that flattered her delicate, heart-shaped face. "Pink daffodils are pretty special, but we found a few for your hat because you're such a special girl. Do you like it?"

Beaming, Vicki examined the straw creation, gently touching the fragile cups of the flowers. "It's beautiful. Thank you."

"You're very welcome. Now let's try it on."

Once Kate settled it on her head, she secured it with a bow under Vicki's chin. "There. The two prettiest hats for the two prettiest girls on Nantucket."

As she started to rise, she felt a hand under her elbow and looked up to find Craig watching her, his eyes soft with some emotion that did nothing to steady her erratic pulse.

"Thank you for doing that."

"It was no big deal."

"It was for Vicki."

"Kids are easy to please."

"Only if you have the knack."

"You do."

A flash of regret echoed in his eyes, and he shook his head. "Not based on what happened Thursday."

"That's not true." Kate lowered her voice. "I got the story from…" She pointed down to her daughter, who was engaged in an animated conversation with Vicki as they watched the cars go by. "And I caught the end of your conversation with…" She pointed to Vicki. "You handled it well."

"I wouldn't have had to handle it at all if I'd done a better job to start with."

"The important thing is what you do going forward. And from what I can see, you're on the right track."

The smile he gave her was strained. "I hope so." He reached into his pocket and withdrew a small digital camera. "Would you mind taking a picture of me and Vicki?"

"I'd be happy to. How does it work?" She reached for the camera, trying not to let the brush of his long, lean fingers distract her.

"I think all you have to do is push this." He indicated a button. "I haven't had a chance to read the whole manual yet. I lost track of my old camera a few years ago and just got this one this week."

As Kate instructed them to say "cheese," the significance of Craig's comment registered. Most people used cameras to record good times spent with family and friends. To capture moments that could be relived in memory for a lifetime. The kind of moments that made life worth living. His lack of a camera meant that since the deaths of his wife and son, Craig hadn't had any moments like that. There'd been no happy times worth recording—or remembering.

It broke her heart.

But as she pressed the button and captured the image of the smiling, blue-eyed man and winsome blond-haired girl for posterity, she prayed it would be the first of many to come as they began a new chapter in their lives.

And despite the fear that held her back from pursuing a new romance, she also found herself wishing that some of those pictures might include her and Maddie.

As Kate handed him the camera and he tucked it back in his pocket, Craig didn't know how to interpret the wistful softening of her lips.

But she didn't give him a chance to dwell on that puzzle, calling his attention to the girls instead.

"I can't believe how quickly Maddie and Vicki became fast friends, can you?"

"It doesn't take long when people click."

Kate's heightened color told him she'd interpreted his comment far more broadly than he'd intended. And that was okay, he decided. Because the statement was true for all relationships.

Including theirs.

As the vintage cars continued to clatter past on the cobblestone street, Craig thought about his reasons for coming to Nantucket—to reconnect with the sea and his daughter. Romance hadn't even been on his radar screen. Yet the woman beside him was making him rethink his vow to live out his life without a partner.

As the parade wound down, Kate checked out the sky, where dark clouds were massing in the distance.

"Those don't bode well for the tailgate picnic in 'Sconset."

"Were you planning to go?"

"No. This is enough activity for one day." Kate reached for her daughter's hand. "Time to go home, honey. I think it's going to rain."

"I'd offer you a ride, but we're parked at the station. It will probably be shorter for you to walk home."

"You're right." Kate took a step back as the crowd around them dispersed. "See you at church tomorrow, I guess."

"We'll be there. Thanks for inviting us today. I think the girls had a good time. And so did I."

Then, very deliberately, he took a step closer, laid a hand on her shoulder and brushed his lips across her cheek.

Her eyes grew wide, but before she could respond Maddie spoke up. "How come you kissed Mommy again, Lootenin?"

"To say thank you for the pretty hat she decorated for

Vicki." He didn't look away from the emerald green eyes riveted on his as he spoke. Nor did he remove his hand from her shoulder. "And because I like her."

"She likes you, too. Don't you, Mommy?"

A blush rose on Kate's cheeks and she edged away, forcing him to release his hold. "I had your sweater cleaned. I'll bring it to church for you tomorrow." She reached for her daughter's hand. "Come on, Maddie. We don't want to get caught in the rain. Bye, Vicki. Craig."

Without giving her daughter a chance to ask any more questions, she hustled her away.

"What are you going to do with the picture you asked Mrs. MacDonald to take of us?" Vicki asked.

Craig looked away from Kate and down at his daughter. "I'll show you as soon as we get home."

Twenty minutes later, after downloading the photo to his computer, he printed out a copy and perused it, impressed by Kate's photography skills. Their faces took up most of the frame, but a flower-laden antique car was visible in the background, providing context.

"What do you think?" He held it out to Vicki.

She smiled as she examined it. "I like it."

"And now comes the best part." Craig rose from the desk in his spare bedroom and retrieved a bag from the top of a filing cabinet. Opening it, he withdrew a small brass frame and slid the photo inside. Then, leading the way, he ceremoniously placed it front and center on his dresser, moving the other picture to the side.

The happy smile on his daughter's face told him that, for once, he'd done something right.

"It looks good there, Daddy."

"I agree. But you know what's even better?"

She tipped her head. "What?"

"This." He swooped down, scooped her up, and twirled her around, cradling her in his arms as she shrieked and giggled.

When he stopped, she threw her arms around his neck and uttered the four sweetest words he'd heard in years.

"I love you, Daddy."

As her phone rang on Sunday night, Kate set aside the manuscript she was editing on the dining room table, grateful for the interruption. She hadn't made much progress anyway since putting Maddie to bed. She was so exhausted the words kept blurring on the page.

Retrieving the portable phone from the kitchen counter, she stifled a yawn as she answered.

But she woke up fast when a mellow baritone voice responded to her greeting.

"Kate, it's Craig. I looked for you at church, but Edith told me you stayed home because Maddie had an asthma attack last night. I thought I'd call and see how she was doing."

Kate's heart was warmed by his concern as she wandered back into the living room and sank onto the couch. "Thanks for checking. It was a bad one. And she had another episode this morning. All in all, it's been a tough day. She's already in bed." She stifled another yawn.

"It sounds like you should be, too."

"I wish. But I have a manuscript due next Friday, and I'm subbing the first three days of the week. I need to put in another hour or two on it tonight."

"I won't keep you, then. But I did have one other reason for calling."

Beneath the studied casualness of his comment, Kate detected a thread of nervousness. It wasn't a quality she'd ever detected in his voice, and she was immediately wary. "Okay."

"If the weather is good next Sunday, I thought I'd take Vicki on a picnic to one of the beaches outside town. She hasn't had a chance to wiggle her toes in the sand yet. Any recommendation?"

She relaxed a little. "Dionis is nice. And it won't be too crowded yet."

"Dionis it is. Would you and Maddie like to join us?"

The invitation caught her unawares. Staring at Mac's painting over the mantel, Kate tried to breathe. "The girls would enjoy that."

"I'm sure they would. But that's not the only reason I invited you. I'd enjoy it, too."

The candid remark was similar to the one he'd made yesterday as they'd parted after the parade. The one that had kept her awake last night during the few peaceful hours when Maddie had been sleeping and she could have caught some much needed shut-eye. The one that was playing havoc with her peace of mind.

The one he'd made right after he kissed her.

For the second time.

As the clock on the mantel ticked, she tried to think. To be rational. Yet her heart kept getting in the way, urging her to accept.

"Kate, it's just a picnic." Craig's quiet, steady voice came over the line. "And if it makes you feel any better, I'm nervous about this, too. I never intended to get involved with anyone again. And I don't think you did, either. But I can't ignore the chemistry between us or the feeling of contentment I have when I'm with you. I've prayed about it, and I've come to believe the Lord led me to Nantucket—and to you—for a purpose. In light of all the hurdles we face, we might end up being no more than friends. But I'd like to test the waters, see where things might lead."

Rising, Kate moved closer to Mac's landscape. Ran a gentle finger over the paint he'd laid down with such care to create the scene of timeless beauty. She couldn't dispute anything Craig had said. There *was* chemistry between them. And like Craig, she couldn't write off their meeting—or remarks like the one about chocolate chip waffles—to simple coincidence.

She, too, was beginning to believe a higher power was at work. And despite the hurdles he'd referenced, perhaps they should take a tentative step into this scary territory. If it didn't work out, if either one got cold feet, they could always revert to friendship.

As she examined the painting that had graced her mantel for the past six years, Kate was suddenly struck by a whimsical touch she'd never noticed before. Tucked into one corner, a tiny mouse was peeking out of its hole, preparing to enter the larger world despite the hazards that might lurk nearby.

Maybe it was time she did the same.

To go for it, as Mac would have said.

Her fingers still resting on the canvas, Kate took the leap. "Okay."

A few seconds of silence ticked by.

"You mean you'll go?"

The whisper of a smile tugged at her lips at his incredulous tone. "Do you want to retract the invitation?"

"No." His response was immediate—and definite. "I just didn't expect you to agree so readily."

"Maybe I shouldn't have. But I can't ignore the chemistry, either. I have a lot of fears to get past before this could ever work, though."

"I do, too. I lost one family to the sea. I have to admit I'm more than a little concerned about getting involved with a woman who spends most of her days on the water. But I'm beginning to accept that what happened to Nicole and Aaron was a tragic fluke. A bad combination of circumstances that would never happen again. I'm not there yet, though. So we both have issues to work through. We'll just have to proceed with caution. Fair enough?"

"Yes. Caution is good. And speaking of caution, why don't Maddie and I meet you there?"

"Sure. If that makes you feel better. About one o'clock?"

"Perfect."

"In the meantime, get some sleep."

She sighed. "Why do I think that will be harder than ever?"

A soft chuckle came over the line. "Join the club. Good night, Kate."

The way he said her name set her pulse tripping into double time again. "Good night."

Returning the phone to its cradle, she tried once again to focus on her editing task. And once again, she found it hard to concentrate.

But this time, fatigue wasn't the culprit.

Chapter Thirteen

The next week passed in a blur for Kate. Between subbing, finishing the manuscript, seeing to the repair of the *Lucy Sue*'s propeller and dealing with another asthma attack, she found herself relying on adrenaline to get her through to the weekend. Her path didn't cross once with Craig's, though she did manage to finally return his sweater via Edith. But her days were so busy she didn't have a spare minute to think of him.

As she dragged herself out of bed Sunday morning, exhausted and beset by serious qualms about agreeing to explore their relationship, she considered canceling the picnic. But Maddie—and Vicki—would be too disappointed. This didn't have to set a precedent, though, she reminded herself as she grabbed a towel from the linen closet and headed for the shower. If things were too uncomfortable during today's outing, the solution was simple. Don't repeat it.

With an exit plan in mind, Kate felt somewhat reassured. But when she and Maddie arrived at church and she saw Craig and Vicki sitting behind Edith and Chester, she steered Maddie into a pew on the other side.

"Why can't we sit by Vicki?" Maddie's query carried

throughout the church, and the foursome on the other side turned in unison.

Pasting on a smile, Kate waved at the other group and bent down to whisper to Maddie. "Because I don't want you and Vicki talking during the service. We'll see them afterward."

Though her daughter pouted, Kate was glad she didn't put up a fuss.

Despite her best efforts, Kate found it hard to give the service her full attention—reminding her of the first time Craig had shown up at the church.

As the last hymn wound down, she took Maddie's hand and exited. Again, like the first time, she was tempted to flee. But running from her feelings wasn't going to change them. Craig had had the courage to address his head-on, and she needed to follow his example. So she stood her ground.

When Craig stepped out the door a couple of minutes later, followed by Edith and Chester, he released Vicki's hand and the little girl ran toward Maddie. The two youngsters started an enthusiastic conversation while Kate waited for the adults to catch up.

Edith beamed at her as they drew close. "What a perfect day for a picnic on the beach. I'm sure you'll have a wonderful time."

If she'd had her druthers, Kate wouldn't have told the Lighthouse Lane matchmaker about the outing. But the girls had been jabbering about it all week. No way could she have kept it a secret. Instead, she'd done her best to downplay the excursion.

But Edith hadn't bought it. Today the twinkle in her eye was more pronounced than ever.

"We're still on, aren't we?" Craig asked.

"Yes. I should have called this week to see if I could bring anything, but my schedule was crazy. It's not too late, though. Would you like me to pick up a contribution at the store before we join you?"

"No, thanks. I've got it covered."

"We'll see you at one, then." She reached for Maddie's hand. "Come on, honey. We have to go home and change our clothes."

"Wear those cute white shorts with the green top," Edith offered. "That would be perfect for the beach."

Kate shot her a silent back-off warning. The shorts were a tad too snug and the boat-neck top tipped too low for Kate's comfort level. She rarely wore the outfit. And Edith knew why.

"I haven't decided what to wear yet." She directed her next remark to Craig. "See you soon." Taking a firmer grip on Maddie's hand, she led the little girl toward her car.

And as she buckled her in, slid behind the wheel and aimed the car toward home, she wished she felt as much in the driver's seat of her life as she did in her car.

"When is Maddie going to get here?"

At Vicki's question, Craig finished spreading a large blanket on the beach and checked his watch. "In a few minutes, honey. We're a little early."

She hovered close, casting a skeptical eye at the breakers. "Is the water going to come up here?"

Smiling, he sat on the blanket, took off his deck shoes and rolled his jeans up. He'd planned an early arrival for this very reason. Vicki had never been on a beach, and he'd been concerned that the waves would frighten her.

"No. It creeps up very slowly, and then creeps back out again. See that line of shells?" He pointed out the high water mark, denoted by various bits of refuse from the sea. "That's as far as it comes, unless there's a bad storm. And today is sunny. See how pretty and blue the sky is?"

She looked up at the cloudless expanse above her but still cast a wary eye at the water.

Craig unbuckled her sandals, stood and took her hand. "Let's see if we can find some pretty shells."

He led her to the high water mark, then gradually closer to

the water, until a larger wave sent an arc of water high enough to tickle their toes. Vicki squealed and scampered back, tugging on his hand.

Craig chuckled and stayed where he was. Leaning down, he drew a smiley face in the wet sand with his finger. "This is even better than crayons." Edging toward the water as Vicki clung to his hand, he drew the sun. "What would you like to draw?"

She eased closer to examine his handiwork. "A flower."

"Good idea. Let's see you do it."

Keeping an eye on the waves, she drew a facsimile of a daisy.

"Very good," Craig praised her. "That's better than—"

"Vicki!"

At Maddie's shout, his daughter straightened up and took off at a run for the approaching duo.

Craig stayed where he was, glad his dark glasses hid the appreciative gleam he knew was sparking to life in his eyes. Maddie, already barefoot, was dressed in shorts and a T-shirt, like his daughter. But it was Kate who drew—and held—his attention.

She'd exchanged her church clothes for beige capri pants and a green-and-beige striped knit top that showed off her slender figure to perfection. Although she'd restrained her hair at her nape with a barrette, he was enchanted by the few springy curls that had escaped to frame her face. She, too, wore sunglasses, hiding her glorious green eyes, but she could do nothing to disguise the soft, appealing curve of her lips.

As they drew close, Maddie grinned and waved. "Hi, Lootenin."

"Hello, Maddie."

Showing no compunction about getting close to the water, she scampered straight toward the breakers, splashing through the waves as they washed over her feet. Emboldened by her friend's confidence, Vicki fell in behind her.

"Don't get too wet, Maddie," Kate called.

Busy dodging waves, the youngster didn't acknowledge the directive.

"Good thing I brought a change of clothes." Kate shook her head and set down the kid-size pails and shovels she'd been lugging. Shrugging the large beach bag from her shoulder, she let it drop to the sand beside the blanket he'd spread.

"I should have brought an extra set of clothes, too."

Kate dismissed his concern with a wave. "Vicki will be fine. I'm just overprotective about Maddie because of the asthma." Kicking off her flip-flops, she sat on the blanket and gestured toward the large brown bag and small cooler on one edge. "What's for lunch?"

He dropped down beside her. "I went to Something Natural and got sandwiches and cookies. I hope that's okay."

"Perfect." A soft smile touched the corners of her lips. "Mac and I used to do this a lot. Pick up sandwiches and head for the beach."

"He sounds like he was a great guy." Craig didn't especially want to talk about Kate's husband, but if anything was going to develop between them they had to get comfortable with each other's pasts.

She fixed her eyes on the distant horizon. "He was. Every day with Mac was an adventure. And special days were amazing. One year on my birthday he enlisted Edith's help and scoured the local gardens to fill the house with flowers so we could have a picnic in a garden despite the rain.

"But my favorite birthday was the year he set up a formal dinner on the beach at Great Point, complete with white linen tablecloth, china and silver. He even rented a tux, and we danced barefoot in the sand while some of his musician friends entertained us."

"Wow." He would never in a million years have thought of such a romantic gesture, Craig acknowledged in dismay. "That's a hard act to follow."

She took off her sunglasses, letting him see into her eyes—and her heart. "Everyone has their own gifts to offer and is special in their own way, Craig. Just like you told Vicki."

His throat tightened, and he touched her hand. "Thanks."

"Mommy, I'm hungry. When are we eating?"

The girls ran up, their feet spraying sand in all directions. He withdrew his hand, and Kate brushed the grains off the blanket as he reached for the bag.

"How about now?"

"Now is good," Vicki declared, plopping down.

As Craig unpacked the food and Kate distributed it, the girls chattered, ending the adult conversation. But once the meal was over and they scampered off with buckets and pails to build a sand castle, calm descended again.

After stowing the remains of their lunch in the cooler, Craig stretched his legs out in front of him, crossed them at the ankles and leaned back on his palms as he watched the little girls.

"I think I've discovered the nation's untapped energy source."

Chuckling, Kate stifled a yawn. "The Energizer Bunny has nothing on kids, that's for sure. I wish I could tap into it."

He took in the faint shadows under her eyes, the weariness at their corners. "You look tired."

"Busy week."

"Why don't you stretch out and rest for a few minutes? I'll watch the girls."

She caught her lower lip in her teeth, obviously tempted. "That wouldn't be very polite."

"Kate, we're not teenagers on a first date. You don't have to dazzle me with your sparkling wit or keep me entertained every minute. I'm content just to share the afternoon with you."

"If you're sure…"

"I'm sure."

Capitulating, Kate pulled a rolled-up beach towel from

her bag, stretched out and positioned it under her head. "I just need ten minutes."

"Take as long as you like. I'll enjoy the scenery."

Five minutes later, based on her even breathing, Craig knew Kate had fallen into a sound sleep. And as he'd told her, he took the opportunity to enjoy the view.

Of her.

In slumber, she appeared younger and more vulnerable, he reflected, tracing the graceful curve of her cheek and the dusting of freckles on her nose. Sleep had wiped the tension from her features, erased the faint furrows of worry that often marred her brow. A slight breeze played with the unruly curls around her face, and he wondered if they were as soft as they looked.

Now wasn't the time to find out, he told himself, tamping down the temptation to reach over and touch one. Not while she was sleeping. But before this day ended, Craig intended to satisfy his curiosity.

A child's shriek tugged Kate back from the depths of oblivion. It was Maddie!

Struggling to rouse herself, Kate tried to sit up. But a gentle, firm hand pressed her back.

"Maddie needs me!" She fought against the restraint.

"Relax, Kate. She's fine. They're trying to catch a seagull." Craig's voice.

Blinking, she shaded her eyes and waited for the last vestiges of sleep to vanish. They were on a picnic. On the beach. He was watching the girls while she took a quick rest.

Except she had a feeling it hadn't been quick.

"How long did I sleep?"

"Forty-five minutes."

Embarrassment warmed her cheeks, and she sat up. "Sorry 'bout that."

"No problem. I wasn't bored."

She shoved a few loose tendrils of hair back from her face, uncertain how to interpret that comment. "Kids are better than TV in terms of entertainment value," she ventured.

"So are other things." He took off his dark glasses, giving her a glimpse into eyes that had darkened in color and grown restless as the sea before a storm. "You're very beautiful when you sleep."

Her heart slammed against her rib cage and her breath lodged in her throat. Though she tried for a teasing tone, she couldn't quite pull it off. "Not so much when I'm awake, huh?"

"Even better then."

He reached over and captured one of her curls, working it between his fingertips as a slow smile lifted his lips. "Just as soft as I expected."

Kate cast a quick glance at the girls, who were engrossed in digging a moat around their castle.

"They've seen me kiss you before, Kate."

Her gaze jerked back to his. This time his meaning was crystal clear.

He intended to kiss her.

And this wasn't going to be a casual peck on the cheek.

But he was warning her. Giving her a chance to back off. Leaving the decision up to her.

She'd known when she accepted his invitation that this was a date. Had known it would move their relationship to a new level. This was a logical next step. And she'd thought she was ready for it. Thought she could get past her fear enough to explore the attraction between them.

Now she wasn't certain.

As if sensing her dilemma, Craig angled toward her and reached for her hand, enfolding it in his.

Staring down at his strong, lean fingers, she went absolutely still as a sudden, overwhelming rush of long-absent emotions spilled over her. For the first time since Mac died, she felt safe. Secure. Protected. Cared for. Wanted.

"If it's any consolation, Kate, I'm as nervous about it as you are. I haven't been on a date in years."

His candid admission did more to quell the butterflies in her stomach than anything else he could have said or done. "I don't want to rush."

"Me, neither. But I think we're past the kiss-on-the-cheek stage, don't you?" A hint of humor diluted the stronger, more intimidating emotion in his eyes, and her comfort level edged up another notch.

"I guess so. But...I'm really out of practice."

"That makes two of us. What do you say we brush up on our skills?"

Without waiting for her to respond, he leaned closer, erasing the distance between them. Cupping the back of her head with his hand, he captured her lips in a gentle kiss that left her heart pounding harder than the surf.

Backing off a few inches, he smiled down at her. "Not bad, considering we're both rusty."

It took her a few moments to find her voice. "Yeah." It was all she could manage.

He grinned and winked. "And it will only get better with practice."

His comment did nothing to slow her racing pulse.

A sudden gust of wind whipped past, stirring the sand around them, and Craig scanned the sky. "We timed this outing well. Looks like Mother Nature is being fickle."

Weather. He was talking about the weather, Kate realized. Forcing herself to switch gears, she checked out the dark clouds gathering on the horizon. But she doubted the tempest to come would hold a candle to the one raging in her heart.

Leaning past Craig, she called out to the girls. "Maddie! Vicki! We need to leave. It's going to rain."

As she reached for her flip-flops, Craig gathered up the remnants of their picnic and rose to fold up the blanket. The girls trotted over, and Kate collected their buckets and shovels.

"Before we go, how about I take a picture of you three ladies over by the water?" Craig pulled his camera out of his pocket.

"Okay." Vicki grabbed Maddie's hand and pulled her closer to the breakers.

Kate held back. "Why don't you just take a shot of the girls, Craig? It would be a nice keepsake for them and—"

"Would you folks like me to take a shot of all of you together?"

An older man and his wife, beach chairs and towels in hand, stopped beside them on their trek to the parking lot from farther down the beach.

Craig took her hand. "I like that idea."

It was like a family shot, Kate thought. The very thing she'd found herself wishing for at the Daffodil Festival. But now she hesitated.

"Come on, Mommy!" Maddie called. "We can all squeeze together."

"Yeah." Craig grinned and gave her another wink. "I'm a good squeezer."

Capitulating, Kate let him lead her over to the girls.

As they took up a position behind their daughters, Craig placed one hand on Vicki's shoulder and draped his arm around Kate.

"Say 'cheese!'" the older man instructed.

After they complied, he examined his handiwork on the tiny screen as Craig rejoined him. "Nice-looking family," he remarked, handing it back. "You folks have a good day." With a wave, he and his wife continued down the beach toward the sandy path that would take them to the parking lot.

Tucking the camera in his pocket, Craig retrieved the cooler and blanket while Kate slung the beach bag over her shoulder and nested the buckets. As they began their trek toward their cars, Craig once more claimed her hand in a warm clasp, entwining his fingers with hers.

It was slow going through the deep, loose sand, and more than once Kate felt off balance.

But while she tried to blame her unsteadiness on the terrain, in her heart she knew it had nothing to do with the shifting grains beneath her feet and everything to do with the shifting landscape of her world.

"I like that picture, Daddy." Vicki watched, four hours later, as the shot of the four of them on the beach emerged from Craig's printer.

Lifting it, he had to agree. They looked like the family the man who'd taken their picture had assumed they were. The little girls—one fair, one dark—were holding hands. His arm was around Kate's shoulders, and she was leaning into him. All of them were wearing happy smiles.

"Where are we going to put it, Daddy?"

"We'll have to start a photo album. I'll get one this week." Since acquiring the camera, he'd already taken more than a dozen shots.

"But can't we put this one where we can see it all the time?"

"Sure. I think I have an extra frame in my bedroom."

"Let's look!"

Vicki led the way, and Craig opened his closet. He thought he remembered seeing an empty four-by-six frame in one of the boxes he hadn't gotten around to unpacking completely.

Pulling the box out, he lifted the lid and dug through it until his fingers closed over the edge of the frame. But when he withdrew it, the glass was cracked and one corner of the wood had been crushed. A casualty of the move, he supposed.

"It's broken." Vicki's face registered disappointment.

Setting the damaged frame aside, Craig was preparing to console her with a promise that he'd pick up a new one tomorrow when the family shot on his dresser caught his eye.

He froze.

No!

Fighting down a wave of panic, he tried to quash the idea that sprang to mind. It was too…final. Letting go was too hard.

Yet how could he move forward if he clung to the past?

"Daddy?"

Vicki's uncertain voice told him she'd picked up on his potent emotions, and he tried his best to summon up a reassuring smile. "It's okay, honey. Daddy's just thinking about something."

"About Mommy and Aaron?"

"Yes. This is a pretty picture, isn't it?" He rested his unsteady hand on top of the frame.

She regarded it in silence. "Yes. But it makes you sad. I think you should put up pictures that make you happy. Like that one. It makes you smile." She pointed to the shot in his other hand.

His daughter was right, Craig conceded. Continuing to mourn for the past would do nothing except deprive him of a future. Nicole and Aaron would always have a special place in his heart, of course. And someday, perhaps, he would be able to recall the joy they shared with fondness instead of pain.

But until then, he needed to set his old memories aside and move on. To open himself to the opportunities the Lord had sent his way to create new memories. With a new family.

Fingers trembling, Craig reached for the koa-wood frame and slid the backing off. Removing the photo, he replaced it with the one taken today, tucking the older one behind it. After sliding the backing on again, he set the photo on his dresser, beside the one of him and Vicki at the Daffodil Festival parade.

A small hand crept into his, and he looked down to find Vicki watching him.

"It's okay, Daddy. You have me."

Hot tears welled in his eyes. Dropping to one knee beside the daughter he'd neglected for too long, he said a silent, fervent prayer of thanks that she'd responded to his fumbling attempts at fatherhood, blessing his life with her sweet, innocent love.

And as he pulled her close, he also prayed for guidance as he entered the uncharted waters ahead.

Chapter Fourteen

Talk about an easy way to make a buck.

One hand on the wheel, Kate guided the *Lucy Sue* slowly through the water off Great Point and watched the three college-age anglers in the stern, who were doing more laughing than trolling. She was glad they were having a good time, but as far as she was concerned they had more money than sense. It was only mid-May, and other than a few premature arrivals, the bluefish were still miles south of Nantucket on their trek north. There was little chance the lackadaisical fishermen would snag even one.

Not that they seemed to care. When they'd approached her on the dock, they'd assured her they were more interested in fresh air and sea breezes than catching fish. And after they'd flashed all those fifty-dollar bills at her, offering to pay more than her usual fee, she'd been glad to oblige. Her cash reserve could use a little extra padding after the expense of fixing her dinged propeller.

Best of all, she hadn't even needed to call on Chester to assist today. For larger groups, he served as her mate. But she could handle three people. Especially when they weren't all that serious about fishing and it was only a two-hour charter.

So far, this trip had been a piece of cake, she reflected, making a wide arc to starboard. It was a glorious, sunny Friday. Perfect for cruising, if not for fishing. And unlike most trips, she had time to enjoy it. After making sure the three passengers knew how to handle their rods, she'd retreated to the helm and let herself daydream about a certain appealing Coast Guard commander.

Since the picnic on the beach last Sunday, her relationship with Craig had taken a quantum leap forward. He stopped in every day after picking Vicki up, sometimes only long enough to claim a quick kiss, other times staying for an impromptu pizza or spaghetti dinner. Those family-type get-togethers were supplemented with phone calls that sometimes lasted far too late into the night. Although her sleep was suffering, she felt invigorated rather than tired.

That's what falling in love could do to you, she supposed. And she was falling. Hard. No question about it.

While lingering traces of fear continued to lurk at the edges of her consciousness, she was doing her best not to let them influence her decisions or impede the progress of a relationship she was coming to believe, after much prayer, God intended for her to pursue.

The brilliant sunlight suddenly dimmed, cooling the air, and she scanned the sky. A few clouds were scuttling across the blue expanse while their grayer cousins gathered on the horizon. Good thing they were more than halfway through this excursion, she concluded. It looked like Nantucket's notoriously capricious weather was about to change. But they'd be okay for a little while.

Kate checked on her passengers. They were lounging in the deck chairs, feet propped up, slugging back the bottles of water they'd brought on board and sharing some rowdy laughs. They still held their fishing lines, but it was apparent their attention was elsewhere.

Turning away from the trio, Kate swung the *Lucy Sue* to port and drank in the view of the cerulean waters ahead. The hue was a perfect match for Craig's eyes, she thought dreamily. Maybe she was a little old for schoolgirl fantasies, but around him she felt—

The sudden sound of a reel spinning out of control refocused Kate's attention and she swung around. One of the college guys vaulted to a standing position, his feet hitting the deck with a thump.

"Hey! I've got a fish!"

Putting the engine in neutral, Kate was preparing to join the threesome and talk the lucky angler through the landing when a larger-than-usual swell rocked the *Lucy Sue*. Kate had no trouble keeping her footing, but the next thing she knew the fisherman standing in the stern lost his balance, staggered toward the rail—and went into the drink headfirst.

The turn of events was so fast—and so unexpected—it took Kate a couple of seconds to process it. Never, in all her years of charter fishing, had she had a customer fall overboard.

His two companions reacted with hilarity. Hooting with laughter, they, too, rose and leaned over the edge of the boat.

"Hey, Marcus, you're not supposed to go in after the fish!" one of them called.

The wind had picked up, and the deck of the *Lucy Sue* tilted as another swell rolled by. Still laughing, the two guys staggered and grabbed the rail.

Snagging a life preserver, Kate elbowed them aside. Their friend was flailing in the water, bobbing up and down, and she heaved the preserver in his direction. "Is he a good swimmer?"

"Sure," one of the guys responded. He swayed toward her and grinned. "In the country club pool anyway."

As his breath hit her in the face, a chill ran up Kate's spine. She didn't have a lot of contact with alcohol, but she could identify the smell.

Snatching up one of the nearly empty water bottles, she sniffed. One whiff was all it took to confirm the clear liquid inside wasn't H_2O.

Her customers were drunk.

Kate had a rule on her boat—no liquor. Alcohol and the sea didn't mix. Period. She was up-front about that with her charter customers, but she hadn't mentioned it to these three. The trip had been impromptu, and she'd assumed their water bottles contained what the label indicated.

Big mistake.

Another swell rocked the boat. As the college kids tottered again, panic washed over her.

"You two, sit down! Now!"

"We can see the fun better from here." His words slurring, the sandy-haired guy gave her a stupid grin.

She looked out at their friend in the water. He was still floundering. Still trying without success to grab the buoyant ring. If he was as drunk as his friends were, he was in big trouble. The water was cold, the wind was rising and, based on his inability to grab the life preserver, she figured the alcohol had seriously impaired his coordination.

Moving in close to the other two, Kate drew herself up to her full five-foot-three inches. Her short stature was no match for their six-foot-plus frames if they balked at her orders, but she hoped her authoritative manner would convince them to comply.

"Look. I can get your friend back aboard. But if one of you falls in, too, you could drown. That's what happens to drunk people in the water. They drown. Is this the day you want to die?" She enunciated each word.

Her serious, intent demeanor seemed to register with the dark-haired customer.

"Come on, Stephen." He pulled his friend back from the railing and tried to push him into a chair.

"I wanna stay and watch the fun."

"Come on!" Pulling harder, he forced him down. Then he took his own seat.

That problem taken care of, Kate redirected her attention to the man overboard. He was treading water, but his efforts were slowing. If Chester was aboard, she could have had him maneuver the boat much closer to the victim while she shouted directions. As it was, she couldn't risk moving in too tight for fear of hitting him. And the two jerks sitting in the stern would be of no help in guiding her. For all she knew, they were seeing double. The best she could do was try to position the boat a few feet away from the victim.

Kate accomplished that maneuver as quickly as she could and put the engine in neutral. Yanking a life jacket out of the bin, she slipped her arms through and pulled the straps snug, struggling to stem her rising panic as she kept an eye on Marcus. It was obvious he was tiring.

Unlatching the fish door in the stern, she dropped to one knee. "Marcus! Marcus, over here." She waved her hands to catch his attention. "Grab the life preserver. It's to your left." If he could latch on to it, she could tow him back with the nylon rope that secured it to the boat. *Please, Lord, let him be able to grab it!*

He tried. But when she pulled on the rope he lost his grip. And disappeared under the gray swells.

Kate's heart stopped.

By the time his head reappeared three seconds later, she'd already kicked off her shoes and slipped into the cold water.

The breath-stealing shock wasn't unexpected. The Nantucket sea was never warm, but in mid-May it still retained much of its winter chill. She knew she had to move fast— before the numbing water impaired them both.

Striking out toward the figure in the water, she covered the distance in less than a dozen strokes. When she reached him, his desperate thrashing warned her to proceed with caution.

He was a lot bigger than she was, and driven by panic-induced adrenaline, he could easily overwhelm her as he struggled to save himself.

Approaching with care, Kate positioned herself out of arm's reach—but close enough to grab him if he began to sink. Shoving the life preserver in his direction, she tipped it up. "Put your arms through the hole," she instructed.

Marcus lunged for the lifesaving doughnut. But he missed the hole, flipping it over—and away—instead.

As Kate reached for it, Marcus grabbed her arm. She wasn't too concerned, figuring if he couldn't hold on to the life preserver, he couldn't hold on to her with one hand. But as she prepared to yank free, his other arm swung around and landed a wild blow to the side of her face.

Stunned by the searing pain that radiated through her head, she gasped. Bright lights exploded behind her eyes, obscuring her vision.

The next thing she knew, Marcus had climbed on top of her and shoved her face in the water, using her life-jacket-clad body to keep himself afloat.

Surrounded by blackness and locked in a death grip, Kate's tenuous hold on rational thought tottered as the danger slammed home.

She could die.

Right here.

Right now.

At the hands of a drunken college student, whose self-preservation instincts were about to cut her life short and rob Maddie of her mother.

No!

The silent, vehement denial ripped through Kate's mind. She wasn't going to let this happen!

Lord, give me strength! she cried in silent anguish. *Please! Maddie needs me!*

Summoning up every ounce of her energy, Kate twisted and kicked and bucked. At first her efforts had no effect. But just when her lungs felt ready to explode, she jabbed her elbow into Marcus's midsection with as much force as she could muster, loosening his grip enough to give her the opening she needed. With a powerful shove, she kicked away from him and shot to the surface.

Sucking in air, Kate took a few seconds to regroup as she treaded water and kept a wary eye on Marcus. Once she could breathe again, she retrieved the life preserver and moved back into position, ready to back off at the slightest indication he was going to lunge for her again.

But he was spent. He was barely keeping his head above water now, and his pupils had gone glassy.

Time was running out.

Shoving the life preserver next to him, she again tipped one end out of the water. "Marcus. Put your arms in the hole." She called out the words, speaking slowly.

Please, Lord, let him cooperate!

She repeated the instruction once. Twice. On the third try, he managed to comply.

The first hurdle passed, Kate let the preserver drop back into the water, over his head. Snagging the attached nylon rope, she issued one more instruction as she began towing him toward the *Lucy Sue.* "Hold on tight."

Buoyed by her life vest, Kate didn't have to expend a lot of energy getting him back to the boat. But no way was she going to be able to haul Marcus through the fish door without assistance. And he was in no shape to climb back on board himself.

With no other option, Kate tried to remember the black-haired kid's name. He seemed the least inebriated of the bunch. Jack, she recalled.

Hauling herself out of the water, she remained on her knees, reeling in Marcus as she issued instructions over her shoulder.

"Jack, I'm going to need some help. Tell Stephen to stay in his chair. You get down on your hands and knees and come over here."

To her relief, the kid did as she instructed. When he crawled up next to her, she noticed he'd gone a few shades paler. Maybe the gravity of the situation had finally registered in his alcohol-fogged brain. She hoped.

"Okay. I need you to grab one of his hands. I'll grab the other. Stay off to the side of the fish door." The last thing she wanted was another headfirst tumble into the ocean. "On the count of three, pull."

Somehow, between the two of them, they managed to drag a spent Marcus back on deck, where he lay like an oversize bluefish—but with far less flopping about. Kate closed the fish door, feeling as if she'd run a marathon. Every muscle in her body ached. And now that the sun had disappeared under a blanket of clouds, the wind cut through her sodden clothes, chilling her to the bone.

Gripping the railing, she pulled herself to her feet.

"Okay. I want everybody below. Jack, there are some blankets down there. Do what you can to warm up Marcus. I'll get us back to the wharf as fast as I can."

After shepherding the trio into the cabin, Kate grabbed her slicker, slipped it on and revved up the *Lucy Sue*'s engines. Turning hard to starboard, she pulled back on the throttle and set a straight course across Nantucket Sound, heading for the entrance to the harbor.

As the wind whipped past, she began to shiver. Partly from cold and exposure. Partly from reaction. But mostly from anger.

Thanks to irresponsible behavior, lives could have been lost today. Including hers. And drowning at the hands of a drunk wasn't in her plans.

But if the incident angered her, it also reminded her that God made the choices about when and how a life ended. And they didn't always mesh with human plans. He'd taken Mac in a way no one had expected—and far sooner than anyone would have chosen. Today, He could have called her home. Instead, He'd spared her. Perhaps because there was more He wanted her to do. More He wanted her to experience.

And maybe part of that *more* was Craig, she speculated as Brant Point Light and the Coast Guard station came into sight. Maybe today's incident was a wake-up call. A reminder that fear and worry don't change the future; they only rob today of joy.

As she eased into her slip on Straight Wharf, Kate mulled over that thought. If she let fear hold her back, she could avoid the pain of loss. But she would also eliminate the transforming grace of love that made life worth living.

She'd known that grace once, with Mac. And despite the hole his death had left in her life, if she had it to do again— knowing her time with him would be short—she'd still marry him. He'd enriched her life in immeasurable ways.

Shaking from the cold and fumbling with the lines as she secured them to the cleats on the pier, Kate reached a decision. She was going to vanquish fear and remain open to the possibilities with Craig.

And she intended to tell him that.

Just as soon as she got out of these wet clothes, downed some aspirin to dull the throbbing pain on the right side of her face and put some ice on the eye that had swollen half shut during her enlightening ride home in the *Lucy Sue*.

Chapter Fifteen

As Craig exited the Hy-Line Cruises office after a meeting to discuss new passenger safety regulations, he paused to scan Straight Wharf. With the high season poised to begin in earnest, the slips were filling up and far more people were milling about than the day he'd first come down here a few weeks ago to tell Kate he was rescinding her safety citation.

The thought of her brought a smile to his face—for two reasons. First, he just liked thinking about her. But second, the irony of their situation struck him as humorous. If someone had told him a few weeks ago that he was going to find himself falling in love with the red-haired spitfire who'd stormed into his office, he'd have laughed.

God, it seemed, had a sense of humor about such things.

As he started to turn away, his smile still in place, a glimpse of red hair caught his eye. Kate. She must have taken a spin in the *Lucy Sue,* he assumed as he watched her secure a line to her finger pier.

But something didn't look quite right.

His smile faded as he squinted at the distant figure, trying to determine what was wrong with the picture. Her movements were rather stiff, he noted, as she rose. And her hair was wet. Not damp and frizzy from salt spray, but dripping wet. As if she'd just been caught in a downpour.

Since that explanation seemed unlikely, he came to the only other reasonable conclusion.

She'd taken an unplanned dip in the ocean.

Craig doubted she'd fallen overboard. Kate was experienced on the water. And she was careful. Besides, the sea was fairly placid, despite the dark clouds accumulating overhead. Could she have had another problem with the *Lucy Sue?*

As he pondered her drenched condition, she shifted position, giving him a side view of her face. And despite the distance, he couldn't miss the discolored skin.

She was injured.

His pulse tripping into double time, Craig changed direction and strode down Straight Wharf toward the *Lucy Sue,* keeping Kate in sight. He saw her gesture toward the cabin of her boat, and though he was too far away to hear what she was saying, the rigid profile of her jaw and her taut posture communicated anger.

The situation looked volatile, and Craig lengthened his stride, watching as three figures emerged onto the deck. Two were attired in shorts and T-shirts, and the third was wrapped in a blanket. They started to approach the stern, and Kate waved them back. Now he could make out her words.

"Stay on deck until I have the boat secure!"

The underlying shakiness in her words unnerved him. She sounded close to losing it.

As the three young men moved toward the stern again, she raised her voice. "I said stay back! I'm not fishing anyone else out of the drink, okay?"

That explained her drenched condition. She'd taken these three guys out and one of them had fallen in, Craig concluded.

But it didn't explain her bruises.

As she turned toward him to secure the last line, the

straight-on view chilled him. Her right cheek was puffy and discolored, and her eye was swollen more than half shut.

Breaking into a jog, Craig drew up beside the boat as she tightened her last knot and rose.

"Craig!" She took an involuntary step back, and he reached out to steady her. "What are you doing here?"

"I had some business on Straight Wharf and I saw you in the distance. What's going on?" Without releasing her, he shot a narrow-eyed look at the three young men in the boat.

She shoved her wet hair back with a trembling hand. "These customers brought along bottles of water. Only it wasn't water. By the time I figured that out, they were drunk. One of them fell in. I had to go in after him."

"What happened to your face?" His stomach clenched as he examined her bruised skin and puffy eye.

"He tried to use me as a flotation device."

As a rescue swimmer, Craig had dealt with more than his share of panicked people in the water. He'd seen otherwise-loving husbands practically drown their wives trying to stay afloat. He'd seen scrawny people develop superhuman strength when faced with their own demise. He'd had to fight off adrenaline-empowered victims who'd clung to him with such ferocity they'd put not only their life, but also his, in danger.

Those situations were covered in rescue-swimmer training. Still, it was a dangerous situation. A terrorized person, no matter how puny, could sometimes overcome even a strong, well-trained swimmer.

And the guy with the blanket draped over him wasn't puny by a long shot, Craig noted. Topping six feet, he had the build of an athlete.

Leading Craig to the obvious conclusion.

He could have killed Kate.

Based on the tremors his hand was absorbing, she'd come

to the same conclusion, Craig deduced. Nor was her shaking being helped by the cooling air and growing wind.

His training kicked in, and Craig switched to official mode. "Do you have a change of clothes in the cabin?"

"Yes." Her teeth were beginning to chatter.

Stepping down into the boat, he held out his hand to her. "Put them on."

"I can ch-change when I g-get home."

"You need to do it now, Kate. You know better than to stay in wet clothes with the temperature dropping." He gentled his voice, but he didn't back down.

To his relief, she didn't argue. She placed her ice-cold hand in his and, with his support, reboarded.

He waited until she pulled the cabin door shut behind her. Then, planting his fists on his hips, he leveled a cold, hard glare at the three offenders, blocking their exit.

"How old are you?"

"We're all over twenty-one," the dark-haired kid responded.

"Let's see your driver's licenses."

They fished them out, and Craig scanned the dates of birth. Too bad he couldn't get them for underage drinking. They were legal—barely. But he didn't intend to let him simply walk away. Not after hurting Kate. Not after what could have happened.

Taking a notebook out of his pocket, he jotted down the information from their licenses. Then he folded his arms across his chest and pinned them with a scathing look until they squirmed and dropped their gazes.

"Let me tell you *boys* something. Alcohol and water don't mix. You—" he pointed to the kid draped in the blanket "—could be dead. So could the captain. Did you get a good look at her face? You hit her hard enough to knock her out. I don't think I have to tell you where you'd be if you had.

"As for you two—" he addressed the victim's buddies

"—if Captain MacDonald had been overcome by your friend here, and you'd decided to play hero, trust me. All three of you would probably be fish bait."

The dark-haired kid swallowed. Hard. The middle one cringed. The one wearing the blanket blanched.

Good, Craig thought. Point made.

"In case you boys don't know, I'm with the U.S. Coast Guard. We risk our lives every day to save people who get in trouble on the water. But we don't have a lot of patience for stupidity."

Craig's dressing down had a sobering effect on the trio. When the dark-haired kid spoke, he sounded contrite—and lucid.

"We're really sorry about this, sir."

"We didn't mean to cause any problems. We were just celebrating the end of the semester and…well…I guess we got a little carried away," said the kid in the blanket.

"We'll pay for any damages," the third one offered.

"Money doesn't fix everything." He folded his arms across his chest again. "But it will help with her medical expenses. Her next stop is the E.R. I presume you boys will cover that."

"No problem," the dark-haired one said.

"I've got your addresses. Give me some phone numbers, including cells."

As they complied, Craig jotted them down. Tucking the notebook back in his uniform pocket, he jerked his head toward the pier. "I suggest you go home and sleep it off. And you—" he addressed the kid in the blanket, snagging it from around his shoulders as he spoke "—get out of those wet clothes. I assume I don't have to tell you not to drive."

"We walked down from the hotel," the dark-haired kid said.

"Good." Stepping aside, he allowed them to scramble out of the boat. They took off down the wharf at a trot, disappearing from view in seconds.

That's when his own reaction set in.

Grasping the rail with both hands, Craig forced himself to take several slow, deep breaths as he faced the truth.

Kate could have drowned today.

Just like Nicole and Aaron.

The very thing he'd convinced himself could never happen again had almost happened. History had come close to repeating itself.

His original instinct—to avoid getting involved with a woman who made her living on the sea—had been sound after all, he conceded grimly.

But it was too late for second thoughts now. She'd already invaded his life—and his heart. Like it or not, they were involved.

How was he supposed to deal with that?

"Craig?"

At the summons, he turned. Kate had emerged from the cabin, but she looked shakier than before as she clung to the edge of the door.

"I checked out my face in the mirror. I wish I hadn't." She tried to smile, but couldn't pull it off. "Wow! What a shiner."

Craig moved beside her and took her upper arms in a gentle grip. Angling her toward the light, he inspected the bruises marring her creamy skin, his gut clenching. "Are you hurt anywhere else?"

"No."

He ran his fingers lightly over the swelling on her cheek. "This needs medical attention."

"They're just bruises." She tried to pull away. "I'll heal."

He didn't relinquish his hold. "I'm taking you to the E.R."

"No way."

"Come on, Kate. It's better to be safe. You might have damage to your eye. Or facial fractures. Did you black out?"

"No." Her breath hitched. "But I thought…he pushed my face in the water and…I know he was just scared…it wasn't intentional…but my lungs started to burn and…I kept thinking of Maddie." Her voice broke and tears welled in her eyes. She lifted her hand and swiped at one that spilled over. "Sorry."

Despite her dry clothes, deep, convulsing shudders rippled through her. And when she dipped her head and drew a ragged breath, Craig knew she was fighting a losing battle to stifle her sobs. While he might be wrestling with new doubts about their future, there was no way he could stand here, his hands absorbing the tremors in her body, and not follow his heart.

Pulling her close, he tenderly wrapped her in his arms. With his hand cradling her head, his fingers tangling in her hair, he gently pressed her uninjured cheek to his chest. "You're okay now. Take some deep breaths," he murmured.

He held her until her respiration slowed and her shaking subsided. When at last she eased back, he let her go. "Humor me on the trip to the E.R., Kate."

"I can't. The last time I had to take Maddie there it cost six hundred dollars."

He should have known money was the reason she'd balked. "You don't need to worry about that. Your customers are footing the bill."

Her eyebrows rose. "How did you manage that?"

He shrugged. "The uniform carries a certain intimidation factor. And I expect guilt played a role. As it should." A muscle in his jaw clenched as he regarded her battered face.

"In that case, I guess it wouldn't hurt to get checked out."

Stepping onto the finger pier, Craig extended his hand to Kate. She took it, grimacing as she transferred her weight from the boat to the wharf.

"Are you sure you're not hurt anywhere else?"

"No. Just achy." She tucked her arm in his as they traversed Straight Wharf. "But as long as I can lean on you, I'll be okay."

Her comment was like a jab in the gut. Because while Craig knew he could give her physical support to the E.R., he was no longer confident he had the courage to make the kind of emotional investment that could bankrupt his soul if he loved—and lost—again.

Two hours later, an ice pack from the E.R. pressed against her eye, Kate frowned as Craig walked her to her door.

Something was very wrong.

He'd withdrawn. Not in a physical sense. He'd stayed with her through the whole E.R. ordeal. But he was distancing himself emotionally.

And it didn't take a genius to figure out why, Kate concluded. He'd told her once he had concerns about getting involved with a woman who made her living on the sea. She thought he'd managed to put those to rest in the past few weeks. But today they must have resurfaced with a vengeance.

It was ironic, she thought ruefully, withdrawing her key from her pocket and fitting it into the lock. The very event that had convinced her to move forward had apparently sent him into retreat.

"Will you be okay here by yourself?"

At his question, she turned. "Yes. Other than a few assorted bruises and a world-class shiner, the E.R. doc said I'm fine. And since Edith is going to give Maddie dinner, I don't even have to cook tonight. Plus, she's close by if I need anything." She fiddled with the key. "Would you like to come in?"

He hesitated, and she thought he was going to refuse. But to her surprise, he acquiesced. "Just for a few minutes."

Pushing the door open, she led the way inside. "Would you like something to drink?"

"No, thanks. Let's sit for a minute, okay?"

"Sure."

She headed for the couch; he chose a chair to the right. Not good.

She waited, but when he didn't speak she plunged in. "You're having second thoughts about us, aren't you? Because of what happened today."

He sighed and wiped a hand down his face. "I was going to try to lead up to that a little more diplomatically."

"Diplomacy, as you've discovered, isn't my strong suit." Kate leaned forward intently, knowing the next few minutes were going to shape her future. "Here's the thing, Craig. I'm afraid of loss, too. But despite my grief after Mac died, I wouldn't have wanted to miss one minute of my years with him. So even though relationships don't come with guarantees, I'm willing to explore ours. Because I don't want to spend the rest of my life alone. And lonely. Do you?"

Raking his fingers through his hair, Craig rose and walked over to the French doors. She watched as he stared into her yard. The evening shadows had crept in, and the sunlight was no longer able to penetrate the tall, thick privet hedge that insulated her yard from the world. Anguish chiseled his profile, and he swallowed. Hard.

The predictable, steady tick of the antique clock on the mantel was the only sound in the tense silence as Kate prayed Craig would find the courage to let go of fear, as she had.

But when he turned and walked back, stopping behind the side chair, she knew from his bleak expression that her prayer had gone unanswered. A little piece of her heart shriveled even before he spoke.

"I wish I could get past the fear, Kate. But I watched the sea claim one family. It almost took you today. And it could happen again." His voice choked, and he stopped. "You're out there every day. I don't know if I can live with that worry for the rest of my life."

She folded her hands, gripping them so tightly her fingers ached. "Do you want me to promise never to set foot on a boat again? Is that what it would take to make this work?"

"I don't know what the answer is." Distress tightened his features. "All I know is that just thinking about what might have happened today turns my blood to ice and twists my stomach into knots."

"And calling things off between us will make you feel better?"

At her quiet question, a spasm of pain contorted his features. "Maybe not in the short term. But it might be better this way for both of us long term."

"Better—or safer?"

"Maybe both."

Kate looked at him for a long moment. She wished she could change his mind. But this decision had to come from within. For now, there was little she could do except give him space and time. And hope he saw the light.

Resigned, she stood. "I'll walk you to the door."

She heard him following, and as she reached for the knob, his hand covered hers from behind.

"I'm sorry, Kate."

The breath from his whispered words brushed her temple, and she closed her eyes.

Let him go, a voice in her mind said.

Remind him what he's giving up, her heart countered.

Kate listened to her heart.

Turning, she lifted her arms, put them around Craig's neck and rose on tiptoe. His hands dropped to her waist, and she moved in closer.

"Kate, I don't think this is a good idea."

She ignored him.

Lifting her chin, she tugged on his neck until he bent his head and his lips brushed hers.

She half expected him to pull away. But to her surprise, after a brief hesitation, he drew her close and gave her exactly what she'd hoped for.

The kiss of a lifetime.

After a while, Craig eased back, breaking contact. His blue eyes had darkened to the color of the sea at sunset on a cloudless summer day, and longing simmered in their depths.

"You make it hard to walk away." His words came out husky as his heart hammered against the fingers she'd splayed on his chest.

"I'd rather you didn't."

The strong planes of his face flexed, as if his rigid self-control had been pushed to the breaking point. "I have too many issues, Kate. And I don't want to let this go any further unless I can resolve them." Dropping his hands, he stepped back. "I'm sorry."

"I am, too." She could barely choke out the words.

For a brief second he hesitated. Then he turned, walked out the door and closed it behind him with a gentle click, leaving her alone.

Perhaps for the rest of her life.

Unless she could come up with some way to alleviate his fears without giving up the sea she loved.

Chapter Sixteen

The next ten days were the longest of Craig's life. He went through the motions at work. Paid special attention to Vicki. Conferred with Edith as his mother's wedding plans were finalized.

But his heart wasn't in any of it.

And much to his chagrin, Lillian picked up on that within an hour of her arrival, nailing him with an if-there's-anything-you'd-like-to-talk-about-I'm-available comment.

He'd declined, and much to his relief she'd been too caught up in last-minute arrangements to return to the subject—until the morning of her wedding.

Although the ceremony wasn't until one, Craig had gotten up early. Long before Vicki awakened. To his surprise, he found his mother at the kitchen table, eating an English muffin.

"Too nervous to sleep?" He grinned at her as he poured himself a cup of coffee.

"I slept like a baby. You're the one who looks like he could use a good night's sleep."

His mother might be seventy, but there was nothing wrong with her powers of perception, Craig acknowledged as he leaned back against the counter and sipped the strong brew. "I have a lot on my mind."

"It can't have anything to do with Vicki. She's flourishing. You've done a good job with her, Craig. She seems happy and content."

"Thanks. Having a friend her own age helped, I'm sure."

"Yes. Edith told me all about Maddie. I met that little charmer and her mother yesterday when we settled Harold into the guest cottage behind Edith's house. Or Honeymoon Central, as Harold's calling it." She gave him a saucy grin. "Anyway, I liked Kate. Edith said the two of you are friends."

Pushing off from the counter, Craig stuck his head in the refrigerator on the pretext of searching for the orange juice. He'd been afraid his mother would get an earful from Edith. The two of them had become good friends during the past few weeks as they'd consulted on the wedding. "I see her a lot since Edith watches both girls."

"Hmm." She nibbled at her muffin. "Heather at The Devon Rose said she could accommodate one or two more people for the reception. She's used to serving high tea for much larger groups. Would you like to reconsider inviting Kate and her daughter?"

"No."

She added some cream to her coffee, stirring it until the dark liquid was diluted to the color of rich mocha. "You know, guilt and fear can be very debilitating."

They were approaching territory he didn't want to enter. "Isn't this kind of heavy subject matter for so early in the morning? And on such a special day? Let's talk about you."

"I was talking about me. Who did you think I was talking about?" She gave him a shrewd look.

He'd walked right into that one, Craig thought in dismay as he took a seat at the table.

Ignoring her question, he asked one of his own. "What do you have to feel guilty or fearful about?"

"Your dad's death."

Frowning, Craig shook his head. "I don't understand."

She sighed and picked at her half-eaten muffin. "I never told you boys this, but I always believed it was my fault he died."

Craig coughed on the sip of coffee he'd just taken. "That's ridiculous! He had a heart attack."

"Shoveling snow. He was too old for that, son. But I was more worried about my bridge club ladies falling than I was about his heart. I should have paid the kid up the block to do it."

She blinked and wiped a speck of jam off the table with a fingertip. "After I met Harold, I felt guilty about falling in love again. And I was afraid of loss. It about killed me when your dad died. So I finally took it to the Lord. And after a lot of prayer, I came to several conclusions. No one is perfect. No one can control everything. And fear not only locks us in the past, it denies us a future."

Pushing aside her muffin, she took his hand between hers. "I don't know what regrets you harbor, or what fears are holding you back, Craig. But if I can learn to let mine go and move on at seventy, you can do it at thirty-nine."

Patting his hand, she rose. "And now I have a wedding to get ready for."

Six hours later, in a picture-perfect ceremony under a cloudless sky, Craig watched as Lillian Cole became Mrs. Harold Simmons in front of a small group of family and new friends.

His brother, Steve, stood beside Harold as best man, while Steve's wife, teenage son and preteen daughter clustered nearby. The groom's daughter, serving as matron of honor, flanked Lillian as her family—a husband, plus three boys ranging in age from about eight to fifteen—looked on. Vicki, in a white dress with a pink sash, stayed close to Lillian as the flower girl. Edith and Chester had linked arms.

Only Craig stood alone.

He was acutely conscious of his solitary status as Reverend

Kaizer commended Lillian and Harold for having the courage to begin a journey together at an age many considered too late for new beginnings and pointed out to those gathered that, as Mark wrote in scripture, all things are possible with God.

He was reminded of it again at The Devon Rose as he watched Edith and Chester share a private laugh in one corner, as Harold's daughter and son-in-law gathered their children together for a family photo and as his brother's family entertained Vicki, who was enjoying being the center of attention. Lillian and Harold had stepped into the garden for a few more pictures.

Catching sight of him, Vicki skipped over. Close on her heels was the eleven-year-old cousin she barely remembered from the whirlwind stop his brother's family had made in Washington last year on their way home from vacation in South Carolina.

"Daddy, can I go with Lauren to their beach house?"

"I'll take good care of her, Uncle Craig," Lauren promised.

"We all will." Steve joined the group. "It would be a nice chance for the cousins to get reacquainted. Why don't you come, too? I know we're all getting together for dinner tomorrow night, but we could extend the party for a while today. It's still early."

The last thing Craig wanted to do was socialize. While he was happy for his mother, the wedding had left him feeling melancholy rather than upbeat.

Searching for an excuse that wouldn't sound contrived, he said the first thing that came to mind. "I need to stop by the station and see what's going on."

"Maybe after that?"

"Depending on what I find, sure."

"In the meantime, are you okay with us taking Vicki?" Steve bent down and tugged one of the little girl's pixie locks, making her giggle. "An uncle deserves some time with his only niece."

Craig smiled. "That's fine with me. I'll stop by later to pick her up, if nothing else."

"Goody!" Vicki declared.

As the party broke up and the newlyweds headed next door in a shower of birdseed to Edith's cottage—Honeymoon Central, Craig reminded himself, stifling a grin—he made the short, solitary drive home after a quick stop at the station. Ditching his uniform, he opted for jeans and a cotton shirt, rolling the sleeves to the elbows as he glanced at the photo of him and Kate and Vicki and Maddie.

They looked like a family.

Except that was an illusion.

But it could be real someday. If he could find the courage to put his fears to rest, as Kate had. And if he could make the leap of faith and put his trust in God, confident that whatever lay ahead the Lord would give him the strength to carry on.

And if he couldn't?

The shadows that had returned in the ten days since he'd broken things off with Kate would forever dim his world.

Pacing the small room, Craig felt as if the walls were closing in on him. He needed fresh air. Open space. Wide vistas.

Grabbing his keys off the dresser, he strode toward the garage. Only one place could give him what he craved. The place where his thoughts were always clearer. Where he most often felt the presence of God.

He needed the sea.

Ten minutes later, Craig stepped onto Dionis Beach and scanned the deserted expanse of sand.

No, not quite deserted, he amended, noting the lone figure in the distance, seated close to the water. The lone *red-haired* figure.

It was Kate.

Jolted, Craig stood motionless. What an odd coincidence

that she'd chosen this time, and this place, for contemplation, as he had.

Or perhaps it was more than coincidence, he conceded.

From the beginning, it seemed God had been pushing them together. Kate had made her peace with that. He was still fighting it.

Yet as he stood there in the ebbing daylight, watching the shadows lengthen, restraining the powerful urge to stride down the beach and take her in his arms, he had a difficult time remembering why.

Fear. That was it. He was afraid to give his heart, only to have it broken again.

As he traced her slim profile and watched the wind toss her flyaway hair, the words she'd said the night of the accident replayed in his mind.

Even though relationships don't come with guarantees, I'm willing to explore ours. Because I don't want to spend the rest of my life alone. And lonely. Do you?

No, he didn't. The last ten days had shown him how dim and dreary his life was without Kate to chase away the shadows. She'd flipped on the light for him, just as Harold had done for his mother.

And the simple truth was, he might think he could control how he felt about her. He might believe he could back off and not let himself love her. And perhaps, weeks ago, that would have been possible. But not anymore. Like it or not, she'd already staked a claim on his heart. Even if he walked away for good, Kate MacDonald would be part of him. And he'd feel her loss as keenly as if death, rather than fear, had robbed him of her presence.

His mother had been right, Craig acknowledged. If he let it, fear would deny him the future that beckoned. A future filled with joy and light and hope.

All at once, Craig felt as if a burden had been lifted from

his shoulders. Although his fears hadn't evaporated, they'd lost the power to control his life. The Lord had at last granted him what he'd been seeking for three long years, Craig realized: the gentle, sustaining peace of true rest. Plus a renewed belief that, as Reverend Kaizer had noted during today's ceremony, all things are possible with God.

His heart lighter than it had been in years, Craig strode across the sand toward the woman who was fast laying claim to his heart, the noise of the surf masking his approach.

"Hello, Kate."

She swung around abruptly. "Craig! What are you doing here?"

He dropped down beside her, drawing up his legs and clasping his hands between his knees. She looked as weary as he felt, Craig thought. "Thinking about us. How about you?"

"The same. Where's Vicki?"

"With my brother. Where's Maddie?"

"With Edith. I heard the wedding was very nice."

"It was perfect. Edith is quite the organizer."

Kate's lips curved into a rueful smile. "Yeah." Then her smile faded, and she gripped her arms around her knees. "I was going to call you after the wedding excitement died down. I've done a lot of thinking and praying over the past ten days, and I have a proposition for you. I can't promise never to set foot on a boat again, Craig. The sea is in my blood, and it will always be part of my life. But if my job is a deal breaker for us, I can sell the *Lucy Sue* and teach full-time. Because if I have to choose between making a living on the sea and giving our relationship a chance, I choose us."

As he gazed into Kate's clear green eyes, Craig felt the pressure of tears building in his throat. Knowing how much she loved the sea, knowing how much the *Lucy Sue* meant to her, he couldn't imagine what that decision had cost her. But it demonstrated the depth of her feelings better than any words she could have said.

Turning toward her, he took her hand in his. "I would never ask you to do that, Kate. I wouldn't want to change one aspect of who you are, and that—" he swept his hand over the expanse of sea "—is as much a part of you as it is a part of me."

"You didn't ask. I offered."

"I know. And I can't even put into words how much that means to me. But I've been doing a lot of thinking and praying, too. And I've come to accept that I can't secure the things that matter most. I can only thank God for the blessings in my life and enjoy them today. Because no one is promised tomorrow.

"I've also found the answer to that question you asked me the night of the accident. No, I don't want to spend the rest of my life alone and lonely. I'm not suggesting we rush things. Or make any assumptions. But I do think we need to move forward and see where God leads us. And maybe, if everything goes the way I hope it does, you might find yourself with a new first mate. In life, and on the *Lucy Sue*—after a certain Coast Guard lieutenant retires. What do you think?"

Kate closed her eyes, drew in a long, unsteady breath, opened them. And at the tenderness and hope in their depths, at the smile that suddenly illuminated her face, Craig's heart soared.

"That sounds like a plan, Lieutenant. Count me in."

Epilogue

Five Months Later

Kate couldn't ever remember such a glorious October day.

Rolling down the window of her car, she inhaled the unusually balmy air as she followed Polpis Road past the Lifesaving Museum and through the moors and bogs. Life was good. And getting better every day, thanks to the extraordinary man who'd stolen her heart, filling her life with joy and adding sparkle to her days.

Like today.

A tingle of anticipation raced through her. Thanks to Craig, she was going to get a rare inside look at Sankaty Light, the iconic tower that had been moved hundreds of feet from its perch on the edge of a steep and eroding cliff a few years before—a feat that remained a subject of discussion among Nantucketers.

When he'd called earlier, shortly after she'd arrived home from subbing, to ask if she could meet him, she'd dropped everything. Edith, bless her heart, had been happy to keep Maddie for an extra hour.

Stopping beside the chained-off gravel maintenance road

that led to the lighthouse, Kate noted Craig's car parked near the stately column. She didn't know what had prompted his trip out here, but she assumed it was some sort of official business, since the Coast Guard managed all of the island's lighthouses.

A handwritten note attached to the door at the base of the tower caught her attention when she drew close, and she stopped to read it.

"I'm at the top, Kate. Come on up. Craig."

Stepping into the murky space, Kate looked around. The outside of the tower was painted white with a broad red horizontal stripe around the middle, but the interior featured exposed brick. A wire-mesh spiral staircase wound upward. Gripping the handrail, Kate began the long ascent.

As she approached the lantern room at the top, puffing a little after her dizzying vertical climb, she tipped her head back. The floor of the landing below the lantern room was visible now. "Craig?"

"I'm here, Kate." His deep voice echoed through the cavernous tower, but he remained out of sight.

She continued to ascend. The spiral stairs deposited her on the landing, near the metal ladder that provided access to the lantern room. Good thing she'd worn an old pair of jeans, Kate reflected, gripping the rungs.

As her head emerged through the opening in the floor, a blue-coated arm reached down. Taking her hand in a firm, strong grip, Craig helped her up the final rungs.

"Welcome to the top of the world."

Any other time, Kate would have been overwhelmed by the breathtaking view from the eight-sided glass enclosure housing the huge lens that flashed every seven and a half seconds. But at that moment, she only had eyes for the man whose warm, intimate smile set her pulse racing. Attired in full dress uniform, he looked as if he'd stepped off the cover of a romance novel.

"Wow." She gave him an appreciative scan. "Big meeting today?"

"Huge."

Turning away from her, he reached down to the floor behind him. As he flicked a switch, strains of Vivaldi filled the small room. And when he stood, he was holding a spray of red roses.

"For you." He presented them to her with a flourish.

"Wow again." Her heart did a flip-flop as she lifted the velvet petals toward her face and inhaled the heady scent. Music, flowers, a spectacular setting—it could mean only one thing. She hoped.

He gave her a nervous, oh-so-endearing smile. "After hearing about the fabulous birthdays Mac planned for you, I figured I better do this right. Because I want you to remember this moment for the rest of your life. So here goes."

Taking a deep breath, he wove his fingers through hers. "Three years ago, I thought my world had ended. I lost touch with my daughter, my faith and my love of the sea. But then I met you, and like this light that guides lost souls home—" he nodded toward the lens "—you illuminated my life and helped me start down a new path. One I'd like to travel with you for all the days the Lord grants me. Katherine MacDonald, would you do me the honor of becoming my wife?"

The warmth and love and devotion in the depths of Craig's vivid blue eyes took her breath away as joy, radiant and transforming, filled her heart. Blinking back tears, she smiled up at him. "You sure know how to stage a proposal."

"Is that a yes?"

"Yes, Lieutenant Craig Cole. That is most definitely a yes."

Setting the flowers aside, Craig cupped her face with his hands, overwhelmed by a happiness so sweet it tightened his throat. Kate was always gorgeous. But today, backlit by the dipping sun, her hair lent a luminous glow to her countenance that put the powerful beacon beside him to shame.

"I love you, Kate," he whispered.

"I love you, too." The words came out a bit wobbly as she put her hands around his neck, lifted her chin and gave him an expectant look.

A smile teased his lips. "Why do I think communication will never be a problem in our relationship?"

She grinned. "You know what the Bible says. Ask and you shall receive."

"Then let's try out some nonverbal communication."

As Craig lowered his head to claim her lips, he watched Kate's eyelids drift closed. Heard her soft sigh. Felt a tremor of anticipation run through her. Inhaled her fresh, salty scent. And sent a silent thank-you heavenward.

For though it hadn't seemed so at the time, God had smiled on him the day He'd sent Katherine MacDonald storming into his office. She'd rocked his world, shaken his resolutions, forced him to face the tough questions.

But she'd also given him the courage to move on. To reconnect with his daughter. To accept the Bible verse Reverend Kaizer had quoted at his mother's wedding: "For with God all things are possible."

Most of all, she'd given him a beacon of hope that was as steady and sure as the tides. For with her strength, her candor, her deep capacity to love, she'd turned on the light in his life.

And because of her, he knew that all his tomorrows would be lived in sunlight rather than shadows.

* * * * *

Dear Reader,

Welcome to Lighthouse Lane!

Although the tiny Nantucket byway in my new Steeple Hill series exists only in my imagination, the characters who call this special place home—either temporarily or permanently—are dealing with very real challenges. The kind all of us face. Loss, guilt, betrayal, forgiveness, trust, learning to let go of the past…the list goes on. But as they all learn in the course of their stories, faith and love can sustain us through the dark times, lift us up when we're down and offer us the hope of a bright tomorrow. I hope you enjoy watching Craig and Kate make this discovery in *Tides of Hope*.

To learn more about my books, I invite you to visit my Web site at www.irenehannon.com. And please watch for Book 2 in my Lighthouse Lane series, *The Hero Next Door,* which will be released in August 2009.

In the meantime, I wish all of you a wonderful summer!

Irene Hannon

DISCUSSION QUESTIONS

1. In *Tides of Hope,* Kate and Craig's relationship gets off to a rocky start when she storms into his office. How might she have better handled her complaint? Has anger ever caused you to act in ways you later regretted? What were the consequences? What are some techniques for controlling anger?

2. Kate's life on Nantucket is threatened by financial problems. Has money—or the lack of it—ever been an issue in your life? In what way? How did it make you feel? How did you deal with it?

3. Chronic illnesses such as asthma can put a great strain on victims and caregivers. Have you had to deal with this sort of challenge in your life? Describe the situation and how you coped. What role did your faith play?

4. When Kate discovers Craig swimming off Great Point, she asks him if he has a death wish. Later, he acknowledges he may have subconsciously been seeking to end his pain and guilt forever. Have you ever felt so overwhelmed that you lost hope? What circumstances brought you to that point? Did your faith help you cope? What scripture passages were especially meaningful to you?

5. In his grief, Craig shut out his daughter. What are some of the destructive aspects of grief? How can our faith help us overcome them? How can we help people who are dealing with grief?

6. Early in the book Craig acknowledges that his faith has

become nothing more than a Sunday routine—a rote behavior, driven by habit rather than compelling belief. Have you ever found yourself thinking of your faith this way? Does this apply to other relationships, too? How can falling into rote, routine behavior damage a marriage?

7. When Craig tells Kate his story, how does this deepen their relationship? Talk about the reasons openness and communication are vital to a relationship. Why is it important to share what's in our heart with the people we love? What can hold us back from expressing our deepest feelings?

8. Craig has decided he doesn't deserve another chance at love, nor does he want to get involved with a woman who makes her living on the sea. Have guilt or fear ever affected your choices? How? What was the result? What guidance does your faith provide in overcoming these issues?

9. Kate tells Craig that love is a great healer. Do you think this is true? Why? Think of some examples of this in your life. What characteristics of love make it so powerful? How are those characteristics revealed in the love the Lord has for us?

10. The near-drowning incident on the *Lucy Sue* is a turning point for Kate. She finally realizes that worrying about tomorrow doesn't change the future; it only robs today of its joy. Have you ever had a "turning point" moment in your life? Describe it, and talk about the reasons it had such a powerful impact on you. What changes did you make as a result of it?

11. At first, Vicki is cautious around Craig, uncertain he'll stick around and follow through on his promise to be a real

father. What does he do to rebuild her trust? Why is trust so important in a relationship? What happens when trust is violated? What are some techniques for repairing it?

12. Why is the scene where Vicki cuts her hair a turning point for Craig? Why is it important to value each person as an individual and not compare them to someone else? Why is this especially important with children?

13. When Kate begins to fall in love with Craig, memories of her first husband hold her back. Why? What insights does she have that finally allow her to move on? Have you ever faced a similar decision? How did you work through it? How did your faith help?

14. In the end, Kate tells Craig that if she has to choose between making a living on the sea and a future with him, she chooses him. Do you think she made a good decision? What's the danger of compromise? Can it be a good thing—or even a necessary thing—in a relationship?

When her neighbor proposes a "practical" marriage, romantic Rene Mitchell throws the ring in his face. Fleeing Texas for Montana, Rene rides with trucker Clay Preston—and rescues an expectant mother stranded in a snowstorm. Clay doesn't believe in romance, but can Rene change his mind?

Turn the page for a sneak preview of
"A Dry Creek Wedding"
by Janet Tronstad,
one of the heartwarming stories about wedded bliss
in the new collection,
SMALL-TOWN BRIDES.
Available in June 2009 from Love Inspired®.

"Never let your man go off by himself in a snow storm," Mandy said. The inside of the truck's cab was dark except for a small light on the ceiling. "I should have stopped my Davy."

"I doubt you could have," Rene said as she opened her left arm to hug the young woman. "Not if he thought you needed help. Here, put your head on me. You may as well stretch out as much as you can until Clay gets back."

Mandy put her head on Rene's shoulder. "He's going to marry you some day, you know."

"Who?" Rene adjusted the blankets as Mandy stretched out her legs.

"A rodeo man would make a good husband," Mandy muttered as she turned slightly and arched her back.

"Clay? He doesn't even believe in love."

Well, that got Mandy's attention, Rene thought, as the younger woman looked up at her and frowned. "Really?"

Rene nodded.

"Well, you have to have love," Mandy said firmly. "Even my Davy says he loves me. It's important."

"I know." Rene wondered how her life had ever gotten so turned around. A few days ago she thought Trace was her destiny and now she was kissing a man who would rather order up a wife from some catalog than actually fall in love. She'd felt the kiss he'd given her more deeply than she should, too. Which meant she needed to get back on track.

"I'm going to make a list," Rene said. "Of all the things I need in a husband. That's how I'll know when I find the right one."

Mandy drew in her breath. "I can help. For you, not for me. I want my Davy."

Rene looked out the side window and saw that the light was coming back to the truck. She motioned for Mandy to sit up again. She doubted Clay had found Mandy's boyfriend. She'd have to keep the young woman distracted for a little bit longer.

Clay took his hat off before he opened the door to his truck. Then he brushed his coat before climbing inside. He didn't want to scatter snow all over the women.

"Did you see him?" Mandy asked quietly from the middle of the seat.

Clay shook his head. "I'll need to come back."

"But—" Mandy protested until another pain caught her and she drew in her breath.

"It won't take long to get you to Dry Creek," Clay said as he started his truck. "Then I can come back and look some more."

Clay didn't like leaving the man out there any more than Mandy did, but it could take hours to find him, and the sooner they got Mandy comfortable and relaxed, the sooner those labor pains of hers would go away.

"I feel a lot better," Mandy said. "If you'd just go back and look some more, I'll be fine."

Clay looked at the young woman as she bit her bottom lip. Mandy was in obvious pain regardless of what she said. "You're not fine, and there's no use pretending."

Mandy gasped, half in indignation this time.

Those pains worried him, but he assumed she must know the difference between the ones she was having and ones that signaled the baby was coming. Women went to class for that kind of thing these days. She probably just needed to lie down somewhere and put her feet up.

"He's right," Rene said as she put her hand on Mandy's stomach. "Davy wouldn't want you out here. He'll tell you that when we find him. And think of the baby."

Mandy turned to look at Rene and then looked back at Clay.

"You promise you'll come back?" Mandy asked. "Right away?"

"You have my word," Clay said as he started to back up the truck.

"That should be on your list," Mandy said as she looked up at Rene. "Number one—he needs to keep his word."

Clay wondered if the two women were still talking about the baby Mandy was having. It seemed a bit premature to worry about the little guy's character, but he was glad to see that the young woman had something to occupy her mind. Maybe she had plans for her baby to grow up to be president or something.

"I don't know," Rene muttered. "We can talk about it later."

"We've got some time," Clay said. "It'll take us fifteen minutes at least to get to Dry Creek. You may as well make your list."

Mandy shifted on the seat again. "So, you think trust is important in a husband?"

"A *husband?*" Clay almost missed the turn. "You're making a list for a husband?"

"Well, not for me," Mandy said patiently. "It's Rene's list, of course."

Clay grunted. Of course.

"He should be handsome, too," Mandy added as she stretched. "But maybe not smooth, if you know what I mean. Rugged, like a man, but nice."

Clay could feel Mandy's eyes on him.

"I don't really think I need a list," Rene said so low Clay could barely hear her.

Clay didn't know why he was so annoyed that Rene was making a list. "Just don't put Trace's name on that thing."

"I'm not going to put anyone's name on it," Rene said as she sat up straighter. "And you're the one who doesn't think people should just fall in love. I'd think you would *like* a list."

Clay had to admit she had a point. He should be in favor of a list like that; it eliminated feelings. It must be all this stress that was making him short-tempered. "If you're going to have a list, you may as well make the guy rich."

That should show he was able to join into the spirit of the thing.

"There's no need to ridicule—" Rene began.

"A good job does help," Mandy interrupted solemnly. "Especially when you start having babies. I'm hoping the job in Idaho pays well. We need a lot of things to set up our home."

"You should make a list of what you need for your house," Clay said encouragingly. Maybe the women would talk about clocks and chairs instead of husbands. He'd seen enough of life to know there were no fairy-tale endings. Not in his life.

* * * * *

Will spirited Rene Mitchell change trucker
Clay Preston's mind about love?
Find out in
SMALL-TOWN BRIDES,
the heartwarming anthology from
beloved authors Janet Tronstad and Debra Clopton.
Available in June 2009 from Love Inspired®.

Love Inspired

From two bestselling
inspirational authors
comes this uplifting
anthology containing
new stories from two
popular miniseries.
Readers will delight
as romance blossoms
and wedding bells
ring in Dry Creek,
Montana, and
Mule Hollow, Texas!

Look for

Small-Town Brides

by

Janet Tronstad &
Debra Clopton

Available in June wherever books are sold.

Steeple
Hill®

LI87531

Love Inspired.
HISTORICAL
INSPIRATIONAL HISTORICAL ROMANCE

There was nothing remotely romantic about widowed father Samuel Hart's marriage proposal to Josie Randolph—but she said yes. The Lord had finally blessed the lonely widow with the family she'd always dreamed of, and she was deeply in love with her new husband. As they crossed the Western plains, Josie was determined to win over Samuel's heart and soul.

Look for

The Preacher's Wife

by

CHERYL ST. JOHN

Available in June wherever books are sold.

REQUEST YOUR FREE BOOKS!

2 FREE INSPIRATIONAL NOVELS
PLUS 2
FREE
MYSTERY GIFTS

Love Inspired

YES! Please send me 2 FREE Love Inspired® novels and my 2 FREE mystery gifts (gifts are worth about $10). After receiving them, if I don't wish to receive any more books, I can return the shipping statement marked "cancel". If I don't cancel, I will receive 4 brand-new novels every month and be billed just $4.24 per book in the U.S. or $4.74 per book in Canada, plus 25¢ shipping and handling per book and applicable taxes, if any*. That's a savings of over 20% off the cover price! I understand that accepting the 2 free books and gifts places me under no obligation to buy anything. I can always return a shipment and cancel at any time. Even if I never buy another book, the two free books and gifts are mine to keep forever.

113 IDN ERXA   313 IDN ERWX

Name	(PLEASE PRINT)	
Address		Apt. #
City	State/Prov.	Zip/Postal Code

Signature (if under 18, a parent or guardian must sign)

Order online at www.LoveInspiredBooks.com

Or mail to Steeple Hill Reader Service:

IN U.S.A.: P.O. Box 1867, Buffalo, NY 14240-1867
IN CANADA: P.O. Box 609, Fort Erie, Ontario L2A 5X3

Not valid to current subscribers of Love Inspired books.

Want to try two free books from another series?
Call 1-800-873-8635 or visit www.morefreebooks.com

* Terms and prices subject to change without notice. N.Y. residents add applicable sales tax. Canadian residents will be charged applicable provincial taxes and GST. Offer not valid in Quebec. This offer is limited to one order per household. All orders subject to approval. Credit or debit balances in a customer's account(s) may be offset by any other outstanding balance owed by or to the customer. Please allow 4 to 6 weeks for delivery. Offer available while quantities last.

Your Privacy: Steeple Hill Books is committed to protecting your privacy. Our Privacy Policy is available online at www.SteepleHill.com or upon request from the Reader Service. From time to time we make our lists of customers available to reputable third parties who may have a product or service of interest to you. If you would prefer we not share your name and address, please check here. ☐

LIREG08R

Love Inspired

HEARTWARMING INSPIRATIONAL ROMANCE

Experience stories
centered on love and faith
with a variety of romances
just for you,
with 10 books every month!

Love Inspired®:
Enjoy four contemporary,
heartwarming romances every month.

Love Inspired® Historical:
Travel to a different time with two powerful
and engaging stories of romance, adventure
and faith every month.

Love Inspired® Suspense:
Enjoy four contemporary tales of intrigue
and romance every month.

Love Inspired

TITLES AVAILABLE NEXT MONTH

Available May 26, 2009

SMALL-TOWN BRIDES by Janet Tronstad and Debra Clopton
Together in one collection come two heartwarming stories about wedded bliss. In "A Dry Creek Wedding," trucker Clay Preston doesn't believe in love but spirited Rene Mitchell may change his mind. Back home in "A Mule Hollow Match," Paisley Norton has found the cowboy she's been waiting for; she just doesn't know it yet.

A SOLDIER'S REUNION by Cheryl Wyatt
Wings of Refuge

It's been a decade since Mandy Manchester last saw high-school sweetheart Nolan Briggs. She thinks he's become a permanent part of her past until the pararescue jumper literally drops from the sky and sweeps her off her feet. He's ready to make a home with Mandy, as soon as he convinces her to take a leap of faith.

A RING AND A PROMISE by Lois Richer
Weddings by Woodwards

Avoiding her first love and his motherless godchild is essential for jewelry designer Abby Franklin. Not an easy task now that Dayne Woodward rejoined his family business, where she just happens to work. But in spite of her resolution, Abby just can't seem to keep herself from opening her heart to little Ariane— and Dayne.

HIS FOREVER LOVE by Missy Tippens
Bill Wellington is sure that his granny belongs in Boston with him. But her hopping social life, and Lindsay Jones, her caregiver, makes him reconsider going home to Magnolia, Georgia. Once he sees her, there's no denying that his high-school crush on Lindsay didn't fade away. Her charms make him long for a second chance at forever love.

LICNMBPA0509